Kate Fortune's Journal Entry

*Heavens me! Thank goodness the family has discovered Tracey Ducet's duplicity. I've known all along that she was a fake and a gold digger—since the **real** missing twin was a boy. I'm thrilled she was caught before she did the family serious harm. My biggest worry now is for Jake. I know he's innocent, and it pains me to watch his suffering from the sidelines. I wish I could help him. I think it's getting time to come out of hiding. My family needs me, and I can't let them down.*

A LETTER FROM THE AUTHOR

Dear Reader,

It's said that you pick your friends but you're stuck with your family. I suppose all of us have thought that at one time or another—some of us more than others—because along with them comes all the chaos families are capable of creating. Unlike many whose own families aren't the most functional, I've been fortunate enough to acquire a marvelous one through marriage. It's a very large, semirowdy bunch, with a dynamic that is fascinating to watch, and a history that could match even the Fortune clan for drama, tragedy and triumph.

Coming from a small family, I find large ones intriguing, if a bit intimidating. So I could relate to down-to-earth, only child Grant McClure's situation, his rueful amusement and amazement at the dramatic family he found himself connected to by marriage. I was delighted to be able to do this story from his perspective, a look at the Fortunes through the eyes of a man who had never really felt like one of them, until an unexpected bequest taught him differently. Adding a heroine I could truly sympathize with, a burnt-out cop who has gone into retreat after the murder of her partner, and tossing in a clownish gentleman of a horse makes for an interesting brew.

No matter what kind of family you have, I hope you're finding the Fortunes interesting and that you'll enjoy this chapter in their saga.

Justine Davis

The Wrangler's Bride

JUSTINE DAVIS

Silhouette Books

Published by Silhouette Books

America's Publisher of Contemporary Romance

To Paiute Mac—
the original clown, and the kind of horse
you never forget.

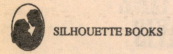 SILHOUETTE BOOKS

THE WRANGLER'S BRIDE

Copyright © 1997 by Harlequin Books S.A.

ISBN 0-373-50186-2

Special thanks and acknowledgment to Justine Davis
for her contribution to the Fortune's Children series.

Printed in U.S.A.

JUSTINE DAVIS

sold her first book in 1989. She followed that up by selling nineteen more in twenty-two months. She has currently sold thirty-two books. She has been a four-time finalist for the Romance Writers of America RITA Award, winning the coveted trophy for her 1991 book *Angel for Hire*, again for 1994's *Lord of the Storm* (a mainstream novel), and again for 1995's *The Morning Side of Dawn*. She has been nominated for numerous *Romantic Times* Reviewer's Choice and Career Acheivement Awards, has won four times and is a six-time nominee again this year. She has also won several RT "WISH" awards for her special heroes.

Justine has been a guest lecturer at UCLA, has been featured on CNN, has been a speaker for various chapters of RWA and has done workshops at several regional conferences.

Justine lives in San Clemente, California. Her interests outside of writing are sailing, doing needlework, horseback riding and driving her restored 1967 Corvette roadster—top down, of course.

Long involved in law enforcement, Justine says that years ago a young man she worked with encouraged her to try for a promotion to a police position that was, at the time, occupied only be men. "I succeeded, became wrapped up in my new job, and that man moved away, never, I thought to be heard from again. Ten years later he appeared out of the woods of Washington State, saying he'd never forgotten me and would I please marry him. With that history, how could I write anything but romance?"

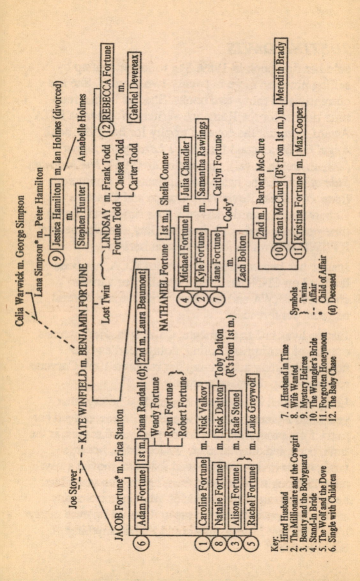

Joe Stover

Celia Warwick m. George Simpson

Lana Simpson* m. Peter Hamilton

⑨ Jessica Hamilton m. Ian Holmes (divorced)

Stephen Hunter

Annabelle Holmes

KATE WINFIELD m. BENJAMIN FORTUNE

Lost Twin

LINDSAY m. Frank Todd

Fortune Todd ─ Chelsea Todd

Carter Todd

⑫ REBECCA Fortune

Gabriel Deverax

JACOB Fortune* m. Erica Stanton

NATHANIEL Fortune   1st m.   Sheila Conner

④ Michael Fortune m. Julia Chandler

② Kyle Fortune   Samantha Rawlings
                              m.
⑦ Jane Fortune   Caitlyn Fortune
          m.
      Zach Bolton   └ Cody*

                    2nd m.   Barbara McClure

⑩ Grant McClure (B's from 1st m.) m. Meredith Brady

⑪ Kristina Fortune   m.   Max Cooper

⑥ Adam Fortune   1st m.   Diana Randall (d); 2nd m. Laura Beaumont

Wendy Fortune

Ryan Fortune }
Robert Fortune

① Caroline Fortune   m.   Nick Valkov

⑧ Natalie Fortune   m.   Rick Dalton ─ Toby Dalton
                                          (R's from 1st m.)
③ Alison Fortune   m.   Rafe Stone

⑤ Rachel Fortune   m.   Luke Greywolf }

Symbols
} Twins
- - Affair
* Child of Affair
(d) Deceased

Key:
1. Hired Husband
2. The Millionaire and the Cowgirl
3. Beauty and the Bodyguard
4. Stand-In Bride
5. The Wolf and the Dove
6. Single with Children
7. A Husband in Time
8. Wife Wanted
9. Mystery Heiress
10. The Wrangler's Bride
11. Forgotten Honeymoon
12. The Baby Chase

FORTUNE'S Children

Meet the Fortunes—three generations of a family with a legacy of wealth, influence and power. As they unite to face an unknown enemy, shocking family secrets are revealed...and passionate new romances are ignited.

GRANT McCLURE: Down-to-earth rancher. He has no use for the opposite sex—especially city women who only want him for his good looks and money. But when he finally meets the woman of his dreams, will he accept that she cares for the *real* him?

MEREDITH BRADY: Endangered police officer. She is the only witness to a crime, and she's forced to seek a safe haven on Grant's Wyoming ranch. Can she overcome her guilt-plagued conscience about her partner's death and find happiness in Grant's arms?

JAKE FORTUNE: Business pressures and his demanding nature broke up his marriage to his devoted wife, Erica. But Jake has seen the error of his ways. Is a reconciliation with his estranged wife possible?

BRANDON MALONE: Monica Malone's adopted son. Following his mother's death, the startling truth about his parentage is uncovered. And this discovery will have repercussions for the Fortune family....

KRISTINA FORTUNE: Pampered princess. She is used to getting what she wants, especially from men who can't resist her sexy charm. Is there any man immune to her beauty and brave enough to tame her willful spirit?

LIZ JONES—
CELEBRITY GOSSIP

Listen up, all you fellow gossips! The scandal couldn't get any juicier! Jake Fortune is in jail. Tracey Ducet—the woman who claimed to be the missing Fortune heiress—is a fake. Brandon Malone is the *real* lost Fortune twin. And most shocking of all, Ben Fortune—Brandon's biological father—was responsible for his own son's kidnapping!

It's true what they say—life *is* stranger than fiction! This is the stuff that Hollywood movies are made of—or at least a good movie of the week. Maybe I should take up screenwriting and submit a script to Brandon, who's trying to break into the big-budget film business. I wonder who will be cast in the leading roles? Do you suppose we could get Harrison Ford to play Jake? After all, he does have experience playing a *fugitive!*

Watching the Fortunes is more entertaining than a soap opera. I, for one, am dying to see the season finale!

One

Was she really that good, or was he just that much of a pushover?

Grant McClure shook his head ruefully as he walked out to the main barn. It was probably a little of both; he'd always fallen in with Kristina Fortune's maneuvers, even when he'd seen right through them. But his half sister was such a charmer, more full of high spirits than of any real maliciousness, it was hard to say no to her.

So he hadn't. And in the process he'd saddled himself with an unwanted guest for the foreseeable future. And at the worst possible time for him, and the ranch.

With a smothered sigh, he leaned against the stall door as he listened to the ranch truck pulling away. Young Chipper Jenkins had been torn, excited about being trusted with the new truck, yet a bit disgruntled at being sent on such a non-cowboy errand to pick up some dude-type woman in town.

"Hey!"

Startled, Grant grabbed at his dark brown Stetson, suddenly canted forward over his brow. He whirled as a nicker that could only be described as amused came from the big horse behind him.

"Darn it, Joker, knock it...off."

He ended the exclamation rather sheepishly as he

heard his own words in the context of what the big Appaloosa stallion had done—gleefully nudged the wide-brimmed hat down over Grant's eyes until it hit the bridge of his nose.

He glared at the horse. The stallion shook his head vigorously, his black forelock flopping over the white patch above one eye, the unusual marking that gave him a faintly clownish look, matching the unexpectedly playful personality that had given rise to his nickname of Joker. The horse snorted, and bobbed his head as if in pleased enthusiasm for the success of his prank.

And Grant's glare became a grin.

"Darn you, you worthless nag," he muttered.

He didn't mean it. The beautifully marked stallion was one of the most nearly flawless horses he'd ever seen. Perfect conformation, power, speed, endurance, he had it all—coupled with a heart as big as the Rockies, a personality that charmed, and the apparent ability to pass his quality on to his foals. The big Appy was any horseman's dream.

And a dream Grant McClure had never expected to come true in a million years.

Thank you, Kate, he whispered to himself, not for the first time. *I don't know why you did it, but thanks.*

"Come on, you big clown," he said, reaching up to rub his knuckles under the horse's jaw in the way he'd learned early on the big animal loved. "Let's get you some work before you go soft on me."

Joker snorted in agreement, and bobbed his head eagerly. Or so it seemed, Grant amended silently, wondering at his continuing tendency to anthropomorphize this animal, something he never did. Except maybe with Gambler, the quick, clever Australian shepherd who was as much a hand on the M Double C ranch as anyone else. But the big Appy seemed to invite the human comparisons, and after a year and a half of dealing with the horse, Grant had finally quit fighting the impulse.

Nearly two hours later, as satisfied as any man could be with Joker's willing, polished performance, he turned the horse out for a well-deserved romp in the big corral behind the main barn. It would make for a bigger cleanup job after the horse inevitably rolled in the dirt, but he'd earned the back-scratching pleasure, Grant thought. Besides, it was late November, and once they'd eaten the Thanksgiving turkey down to the bone, cold weather was generally here for good in the Wyoming high country; soon there'd be nothing but snow to roll in. It was a little surprising that they'd had few storms already, and far enough apart that the snow had time to melt in between.

But it wouldn't be long before the white stuff was here to stay, and lots of it. And then he and all the hands would be working to sheer exhaustion just to keep the stock alive through the Wyoming winter, and the last thing he needed was to have to nursemaid some big-city girl who—

The sound of the ranch's truck returning cut in on his thoughts.

"Here goes," he muttered to himself, slinging Joker's bridle over his shoulder and reversing his steps to go greet his visitor; it had been rude enough not to go himself to pick her up, but he had—perhaps childishly—drawn the line at dancing to Kristina's manipulating tune there.

He saw Chipper first. Standing beside the driver's door of the mud-spattered blue pickup, the young man was grinning widely, his face flushed, and looking utterly dazzled. Grant frowned. And then he saw the obvious reason for the young hand's expression; the woman who had scrambled without help from the high truck's passenger seat. Long blond hair, pulled back in a ponytail, bounced as she walked around the front of the truck. She was wearing jeans and a heavy sheepskin jacket, and was seemingly unbothered by the briskness of the air.

She came to a halt when she spotted him, her eyes widening slightly. Grant knew he was staring, but he couldn't help himself; he hadn't expected this.

She was small, at least from Grant's six-foot viewpoint, and not just in height; from her pixieish face to a pair of very small feet encased in tan lace-up boots, every inch of her looked delicate, almost fragile. And the dark circles that shadowed her eyes only added to the overall air of fragility. She looked tired. More than tired, weary, a weariness that went far beyond the physical. Grant felt an odd tug somewhere deep inside; his father had looked like that in the painful days before his death five years ago.

She was looking at him, that fatigue dimming eyes that should have been a vivid green into a flat dullness.

"Hello, Grant."

Her voice was soft, husky, and held an undertone that matched what he'd seen in her eyes.

"Hello, Mercy," he said quietly.

She smiled at the old nickname, but the smile

didn't reach those haunted eyes. "No one's called me that since you quit coming home summers."

"Minneapolis was never my home. It was just where my mother was."

She glanced around, as if trying to take in the vastness of the wild landscape with eyes used to the steel-and-concrete towers of the city, not the granite-and-snow towers of the Rocky Mountains.

"No, this was always home for you, wasn't it?" she said, her voice barely above a whisper.

"Always."

His voice rang with a fervency he didn't try to hide. He'd known from the time he was a child that this place was a deep, inseparable part of him, that its wild, elemental beauty called to something so intrinsic to him that he would never be able to—or want to—resist.

"So this is what you always had to go back to. I think I understand now."

She sighed. It was a tiny sound, more visible than audible. He'd thought, when Kristina told him Meredith Brady had become, of all things, a cop, that she must have grown a lot since that last summer, when she was a pesky, tenacious fourteen-year-old and the same height as his two-years-younger half sister. She hadn't. If she'd gained more than an inch in the twelve years since, he'd be surprised. She couldn't be more than fifteen-two, he thought, judging with an eye more used to calculating height on horses than on people. Especially women.

"You've...changed," he said. And it was true; he remembered her as a live-wire girl who had looked a great deal like his half sister, except for green eyes in place of Kristina's pale blue, a girl with a lot of energy but not much stature. The stature hadn't changed much, but the energy had; it seemed nowhere in evidence now.

"Changed, but not grown, is that it?" she said, sounding rueful.

"Well," he said reasonably, "you haven't. Much."

"Easy for you to say. You're the one who grew four inches in one summer."

Grant's mouth quirked. That had been an awkward summer, when his fifteen-year-old body decided now was the time and shot him to his full six feet in a spurt that indeed seemed to happen in a three-month span. He'd been embarrassed at his sudden gawkiness and the clumsiness that ensued, and the fact that none of his clothes fit anymore, but even more embarrassed by the fascination the change seemed to hold for his half sister's annoyingly omnipresent best friend.

"Amazing I grew at all, with you glued to my heels, Meredith Cecelia."

She winced. "Ouch. Please, stick with just Meredith. Or Meri."

She gave him a sideways look. He read it easily, and laughed.

"Or Mercy?" he suggested. "Or rather, 'No Mercy'?"

He'd been rather proud of his own cleverness in coining the name for her when they met that first summer so long ago, combining her first and middle names and his own irritation at her tenaciousness in following him around.

"You always were annoyingly proud of coming up with that," she said dryly.

"It fit," he pointed out. "You never would leave me alone. Every time I came to visit Mom, you were always hanging around. I'll never forget that time you followed me to the ice rink and got stuck in the turnstile."

"I was only twelve," she explained with some dignity. "And I had a huge crush on you, after you saved me from those boys who were teasing me."

Grant blinked. He'd guessed she had a crush on him—it hadn't been hard, with the quicksilver girl dogging virtually his every step each summer he came to visit—but he hadn't realized it had started then. He remembered finding her that first summer, cornered by the two bigger boys, her chin up proudly, despite the tears welling from her eyes. He'd chased her tormentors away, then walked her home. She'd said nothing until they got to her house, and then only a quiet thank-you. But now that he thought about it, that was about the time she had become his ever-present shadow.

"They were just a couple of bullies," he said.

"And you were my white knight," she returned softly.

Grant winced; he wasn't hero material, not even for an impressionable child.

"Oh, don't worry," she said, as if in answer to his expression. She smiled widely—a better smile this time, one that almost brightened her eyes to the vivid green he remembered. "I got over it long ago. Once I grew up enough to realize I'd fallen for a pretty face without knowing a thing about the man behind it, I recovered quite nicely. Thank goodness.''

''Oh.''

It came out rather flatly, and Grant's mouth quirked again. Was he feeling flattered that she'd admitted to that long-ago crush? Or miffed that she'd gotten over it so thoroughly? And seemed so cheerful about it? He nearly laughed; hadn't he had enough of women enamored purely of his looks? And more than enough of those who, when they found out there was a comfortable amount of money behind the McClure name, became even more enamored?

At least Mercy had never been that kind of female; even at her adoring worst as a child, she'd never fawned on him. She'd been too much a tomboy for that, an unexpected trait in such a delicate-looking little pixie. A tiny dynamo with a blond ponytail, she'd merely followed him. Everywhere.

She still had the ponytail. But the tomboy had grown up. And there was no denying that the gamine features that had once reminded him of a mischievous imp were now enchanting. Big eyes, turned-up nose, sassy chin...Meredith Brady had become a beautiful woman. A very beautiful woman. No wonder Chipper had looked dazed.

Chipper. Who was standing there with wide eyes and wider ears, Grant thought wryly, listening to this entire exchange. And stealing shy but eager glances at Mercy, who seemed utterly unaware of the eighteen-year-old's fascination.

Which didn't mean, Grant told himself sternly, that he had any excuse for standing here staring at her himself. And the fact that he had been alone for a long time wasn't any justification for the sudden acceleration of his pulse, either. This was the bane of his teenage existence, after all. No Mercy, the pest. Just because she'd grown into a lovely adult didn't mean a thing. Not a darn thing. But he did wonder if she ever let down that ponytail, and how the silky-looking hair would fall if she did.

"Get on those salt blocks," he instructed the young hand firmly. "I'll show her up to the house."

Chipper looked crestfallen. "I was gonna carry her bags up for her—"

"I can manage," she said. "There's not that much. I tend to travel light."

"But I—"

"I need those salt blocks set out," Grant said. "Now."

"Yes, sir," Chipper said resignedly. Then he brightened, turning his freckled face back toward Mercy. "If you need someone to show you around—"

"I'll keep you in mind," she said, smiling at the boy.

An utterly charming smile, Grant thought. And utterly without heart. A practiced, surface smile, reflecting nothing of the woman behind it. Yet it didn't seem to him a phony smile, not like those of some of the women he'd encountered in his infrequent forays into the society his mother was now a part of.

No, this wasn't a smile to hide shallowness, it was more of a mask, to hide...what? Emptiness? Pain?

It came back to him in a rush then, what Kristina had said in her phone call to him last week. It had taken him a moment to connect the name that sounded familiar to the memory of his pesky blond shadow, so he'd missed the first part of what his half sister said. But her plea had been simple enough; Meredith needed someplace to go, a shelter, away from the city, for a while, after the death of her partner, Nick Corelli, who had been murdered in the line of duty.

"She and Nick were very close," Kristina had said, in the most patently sincere part of her wheedling request. "She's devastated. She needs to rest, she's running herself ragged. Please, Grant. Just for a while. She needs someplace quiet, where people won't talk about what happened all the time. Someplace to grieve, and to heal."

That was it, he thought. Grief was what was living behind that careful smile. She must have loved the man a great deal. And here he was overheating absurdly, not only over his childhood nemesis, but over a woman grieving for a loved one. Mentally chastising himself, he reached for the two bags Chipper had set down beside the truck.

"I said I can get those," she said.

"I'm sure you can, but I'll do it. You've had a long trip."

"I sat for most of it," she pointed out. "I can carry my own bags."

Grant dropped the bags, wondering if this was how this visit was going to go. His mother had been at great pains to teach him manners during the few months of the year he spent with her growing up. When he complained that women didn't seem to want manners anymore, she'd quietly told him women *and*

men most certainly did, they just didn't want conde-
scension along with them, and continued her lessons.

He crossed his arms across his chest. But before he
could open his mouth, she forestalled him.

"It's not a gender thing," she said quickly, as if
she'd read his thoughts. "I'm intruding here, I know
that. You have a ranch to run, and you're doing me
a big enough favor just by letting me stay here. If
there's anything I can do to help out, just tell me. I
don't want to be treated like a guest, so I don't want
to start out that way."

He looked at her quizzically. "Then just exactly
how do you want to be treated?"

She smiled suddenly, the most genuine smile he'd
seen from her yet. And it sent a snap of electricity
arcing through him that startled him with its swiftness
and power.

"Ignoring me would be fine."

Despite the unexpected jolt, his mouth quirked with
humor. "I doubt anyone ignores you successfully,
Mercy," he said dryly. "I tried every summer for
years."

She only lifted a delicately arched brow at his use
of the childhood nickname again. "I know. And the
harder you ignored me, the more determined I got."

"I know."

He had to look away from her; that smile was getting to him again. He cleared his throat. He'd warned
Kristina, who had only been to the ranch in the summer, about all this, but she'd insisted that was exactly
what her friend needed. But he didn't know if she'd
passed his warnings on.

"You'll be pretty much stuck inside once the snow really sets in."

"I brought lots of books," she said.

"I don't expect you to work. But I do expect you not to create any extra work for my men. Winter is our roughest season, and the hands will be hard-pressed enough just to keep things running around here."

Mercy didn't take offense. "I probably wouldn't be much good to you anyway," she answered easily. "I've never ridden a real horse, and I know next to nothing about cows. But I can take care of myself. You don't need to look out for me."

"Cattle," he corrected mildly.

"Okay." She shrugged, accepting that easily, as well. Clearly she had no problem admitting when she knew nothing about something. Grant wished there were more people like that; he'd seen too many who came to this part of the country thinking they were going to find adventure, never knowing or even thinking of the realities of the life they were taking on. His stepbrother Kyle had been one of those. But rancher Samantha Rawlings had quickly—and permanently—straightened him out, Grant thought with an inward grin. And he'd done fairly well, despite the fact that he'd never been able to settle down to any job in his life before.

But then, with the manipulative, vindictive Sheila Fortune for a mother, that was hardly any surprise, Grant thought, thankful yet again for his own mother's warmth and genuine goodness. It was amazing that Sheila's children had managed any semblance of lives of their own, and with Kyle, Michael and Jane all married now, Sheila must be frothing at having lost so much control over her children. He didn't envy his stepsiblings at all. In fact, there were times when he even felt sorry for his stepfather, but he usually got over that in a hurry.

He forced himself back to the matter at hand, wondering why he was finding it so difficult to simply talk to this woman, why his thoughts were rambling in crazy directions.

"I won't have time to look out for you, once the snow flies," he warned. "And neither will anybody else. You'll be on your own."

Something dark and painful flickered in her eyes, and Grant regretted using those words.

"I'll be fine," she said briskly.

Her tone belied what he'd seen in her eyes, but he guessed she was only hiding it well. Or had a lot of practice at suppressing such emotions. She reached for one of the soft-sided navy cases.

"Split them?" she suggested.

"Fine," he said, and took the other.

She lifted the bag easily, although Grant knew it wasn't light. He shouldn't be surprised, he told himself. As a cop—especially a female one—she probably had to be more than just strong and fit to hold her own. And apparently she did hold her own; Kristina had told him she'd been on the force five years, graduating the academy and turning twenty-one, the minimum age to be sworn in, on the same day. It was what she'd always wanted, Kristina had said, and once Meredith Cecelia Brady set her eyes on a goal, there was nothing and no one who could stop her.

The admiration in his somewhat spoiled half sister's tone had been genuine, and that was rare enough that Grant had paid attention. And had agreed to her request. Sometimes Kristina could be worse than annoying; only the fact that she was as smart and charming as she was spoiled made her bearable. Someday, he thought, she was going to run into some man she couldn't control, some man who had no patience with her spoiled-princess act, and the sparks were going to fly.

But Mercy had been her truest friend, kept through the years, and when she needed help, Kristina had been there. And she hadn't hesitated to use her half brother to get what she wanted. And since it was one of those rare times when Kristina asked for something not for herself, Grant hadn't been able to turn her down.

Mercy.

She'd told him what to call her, but he kept thinking of her as Mercy, reverting to the old childhood nickname. He wasn't sure why. A reminder, perhaps, of who she was? A friend of Kristina's, and a woman in mourning. He would do well to remember that, and if using that name would do the trick, then he'd use it. He hadn't forgotten that unexpected jolt, or the sudden revving of his heartbeat; inappropriate as it was, it had happened, and if using that childhood name would keep a bit of distance between them, then that was yet another reason to do it. He had no time to deal with that kind of response. He was sure of that.

Just as he was sure it had simply been the result of going too long without feminine companionship; hell, he'd barely seen a woman for a month, and hadn't been on a date in three times that long. No wonder his libido had kicked to life at the sight of the lovely woman Mercy had become. He was sure that was all it was.

He just wasn't sure he knew the first thing about providing sanctuary for a heart as wounded as Mercy's seemed to be. He knew about the pain of loss, he'd known about it for a long time, ever since his mother had left his father and the ranch, when he was three years old. And he'd had it pounded home again when his father died, a long, slow death that had been agony to watch, a strong, vital man wasting away, with his last breath regretting that he'd lost the only woman he'd ever really loved to the city life he hated.

He'd found nothing to ease the pain he felt then. So how could he ever hope to provide it for someone else? He wouldn't even know where to begin. Kristina had said Mercy wanted only a place to hide, to heal, to find peace. While, in time, he had found these things himself in the wild reaches of this Wyoming country, he had little hope that a city girl like Mercy would find the same kind of relief. Especially since she was dealing with such a brutal, unexpected death. The death of someone who, judging from that look in her eyes, she had loved very much.

He wasn't sure there was any relief for that kind of pain.

Two

She might not see that white knight anymore when she looked at Grant McClure, Mercy thought, but he was certainly no less imposing or handsome or rugged than he had seemed to her all those years ago. Working on a ranch did wonderful things for the male physique, things that all the gym-bound men she knew in Minneapolis could only dream about.

And she liked the slight appearance of lines around his eyes, eyes that were clearly used to gazing over long distances, eyes that were even more vividly blue than she'd remembered against his tanned skin. His sandy brown hair was shorter than the long locks he'd worn as a teenager, now barely brushing his collar, but it looked good on him.

He looked good, period, she thought, proud of how coolly she could acknowledge the fact, with none of the flutter that used to seize her as a child every time she looked at him.

Well, almost none.

She stuffed a sweater into a drawer, closed it, then straightened to look around the room. Grant had told her Kristina used it on the rare occasions when she visited the ranch—"before the isolation and lack of parties gets to her and she hotfoots it back to the city." But it seemed obvious that her friend had left little imprint on the place.

Or perhaps Grant had returned it to normal when she wasn't there; the plain, utilitarian furnishings were hardly Kristina Fortune's style. But Mercy felt comfortable with the large four-poster bed, the plain oak dresser and small desk, and the severely tailored curtains that still managed to be cheerful in a bright blue-and-white check. A comfortable-looking arm-chair, upholstered in the same bright blue and sitting next to a large window, completed the simple furnishings.

She walked over to the bed and lifted the small stack of long-sleeved T-shirts she'd brought. Layers, she'd thought as she packed. Kristina had had some choicely descriptive words for winters on her half brother's ranch, even though she'd never weathered one herself. Mercy had smiled at the thought of anyone from Minneapolis finding someplace else colder, but had packed accordingly.

And wasn't it just amazing, she thought as she put the shirts in another drawer, how quickly she'd slipped back into accepting that old nickname? At first, back then, she'd hated it, but she'd grown to like it when she realized that Grant was the only one who called her that, as if it were something special and private between them.

And now, she thought as she shut the drawer, it was obvious that he still thought of her as that child he'd teased. Which was just fine with her.

She turned back toward the last thing on the bed, the two silk nightgowns she'd brought. She might have to wear jeans and long johns and wool socks during the day, but at night she preferred the smoothness of silk. It was one of her few indulgences, so she refused to feel guilty or foolish about it.

She had just tucked them neatly into the last drawer and pushed it closed when an odd scrabbling sound turned her around.

"Well, hello," she said, smiling at the knee-high dog with the mottled gray-and-black coat who sat politely just outside her door. He looked at her steadily, with a gaze that was rather disconcerting, since one of his eyes was brown and one a pale blue. She walked over and crouched before the animal. Something in his demeanor prevented her making any presumptuous overtures, such as patting his head; he didn't seem the type of dog who would welcome instant familiarity.

"Come to check out the intruder, have you?" she asked.

The dog cocked his head, and looked at her so assessingly she nearly laughed.

"I'd recommend you leave him alone. He's not the cuddly type."

She looked up quickly, amazed at how quietly Grant had moved down the hall. She'd barely heard him before he spoke, and she was rarely taken by surprise like that.

"I can see that," she said. "I've dealt with a dog or two in my time. I recognize the look-but-don't-touch signals."

"He's a working dog, not a pet. He's not looking for friends."

For an instant, Mercy wondered if there was more to his words than simply a warning about the dog.

Then she decided she was looking for things that weren't there.

"Then far be it for me to trespass," she said, standing up. The dog continued to look at her, somewhat quizzically now. "But should he change his mind, I trust you won't have a problem if I don't reject him?"

"Not likely," Grant said shortly, leaving Mercy wondering if he was referring to the dog or himself. She smothered a sigh; she didn't remember him being so prickly.

"Does he have a name?" she asked. "Or is he simply 'Dog'?"

To her amazement, Grant flushed. "Er...well, he was just Dog for a while. Until he showed us who he was."

Mercy smiled; what a wonderful way to think of it. "So what name did he earn?"

He seemed relieved, as if he'd expected her to find his answer silly. "Gambler."

Mercy glanced at the dog, who sat motionless in the same spot she'd first seen him in. "Really? Why?"

Grant smiled then. "He's a lazy slug when he's not working. But when he is...he does the work of five hands. And he won't let anything get in his way. You tell him to move cattle, he moves them. Over, under, around, he's everywhere, and they keep moving, as if he were a field marshal ordering his troops. I've seen him move a small herd a quarter of a mile without ever touching the ground."

Mercy blinked. "What?"

"He walks on 'em. Jumps. Steer to steer, cow to cow, whatever. Gambles his life on his own surefootedness. He never stops moving. And neither do they.''

She looked back at the dock-tailed animal, who couldn't weigh more than forty pounds, if that. ''I can see why he has that patrician air, then. He's earned it.''

''Yes, he has.''

He sounded pleased. And for some reason that made her unable to meet his gaze. She looked at the dog instead, until Grant spoke.

''I thought you might like to look around the place. Get oriented.''

She looked at him then, and wondered why she hadn't been able to before; there was nothing intimidating about him now. At least, nothing more than his size and muscle, and she was used to that. And she'd handled bigger men than him in her five years on the force.

''I'd like that. And that way I won't have to bother anyone later.'' She gave him a sideways look. She wasn't sure how much Kristina had told him, and she didn't want to go into any more details than necessary. ''And I promise this will only be for a while. As soon as...they call me, I'll be on the next plane out, and out of your way.''

He looked at her for a moment. ''I...didn't mean to give you the impression you would be a bother.''

''Of course I will,'' she said with a shrug. ''I don't live here, don't know about life on a ranch. I can't help but be somewhat of a bother. But I'll try my best to keep it to a minimum.''

He raised one sandy brow. ''You *have* changed.''

She laughed, realizing as she did so that it was the

first time since Nick had died that she'd really, genuinely laughed. She quashed the instant welling of pain that seemed to always be there, ready to swamp her any time she let her guard down and thought of the man who had been so much more to her than just a partner.

"You mean I never used to care if I was a nuisance or not?" she managed to say lightly.

He smiled, as if her laugh had pleased him. "Something like that."

"Only around you," she said. "And probably only because it bugged you so much."

His smiled turned wry. "I had a sneaking suspicion even back then that that was why you did it."

"If you had really ignored me, I probably would have just gone away."

"*Now* she tells me," Grant said with mock sarcasm.

This time, they both laughed, and Mercy felt a slight lessening of the steady ache she felt as if she'd been carrying forever, although she knew it had been only since the grim night Nick had died in her arms, five weeks ago.

She grabbed up her shearling jacket and tugged it on as they walked down the stairs to the main part of the house. It was a story and a half, in a rambling floor plan which seemed bigger than it probably was, because of the steep pitch of the roof, which was designed for heavy snows. The three bedrooms were tucked up in that well-insulated roof area, to take advantage of the warm air generated by the wood stoves Grant had told her he preferred to rely on.

"We've got propane heat," he'd said as they

passed the big storage tank, "but I try not to use it if we don't have to. Cooking and hot water takes enough."

"Hot water?" she'd said teasingly. "Kristina told me this was roughing it."

He'd given her a long look, as if gauging whether she was serious; she'd realized then that he must really think she was a pampered city girl. She hadn't tried to tell him he was wrong; that wasn't the kind of thing you proved with talk. She'd just keep out of his way and take care of herself.

"I like long showers," he'd said, rather shortly, and Mercy had been disconcerted enough at the unexpected images his words caused to be unable to answer. She'd thought herself long past thinking about Grant McClure that way, but there was no denying that the thought of him standing naked in a steamy shower did strange things to her heart rate.

"Everybody keeps an eye on the fire in here during the winter," he said now, gesturing toward the sizable wood stove that sat on a brick slab in a corner lined with the same brick. "It's easier to keep the place above freezing than it is to get it warmed up from freezing."

She shook off the lingering effects of the unwelcome and surprisingly erotic memory. "I'll bet it is," she said, noting the sizable stack of wood against the inside wall. "Where's the woodpile?"

He nodded toward a closed door a few feet from the stove. "There's a lean-to outside that door. We try to keep enough dry inside to get through a week. If we're lucky, that's the longest whiteout blizzard we have."

She nodded. If he was expecting shock from her at the idea of such weather, he was going to be disappointed. Yes, she lived in the city, but that city was Minneapolis, and she was no stranger to harsh weather. Although as she looked up at the Rockies on the ride out here from Clear Springs, she'd felt a tiny shiver up her spine that made her think that perhaps those mountains had a thing or two to teach anyone about real weather.

"Chipper seems like a nice kid," she said as she followed Grant out the front door.

"He is just that," Grant said. "Nice, but a kid. He just signed on full-time after he graduated high school."

Was there a warning somewhere in those words, Mercy wondered? Or was she again reading things that weren't there into Grant's words? She'd hardly been able to miss the boy's reaction to her, the way he'd blushed and stammered the whole ride back to the ranch. But what did Grant think she was going to do, toy with the affections of an innocent kid? Suddenly the irony of it hit her, and she smiled wryly.

"Lord, did I look at you like that? All cow-eyed and red-faced?"

Grant stopped his long strides and looked at her sharply. Then, slowly, a smile curved his mouth. A smile that hadn't lost any potency in the past twelve years.

"Sometimes," he admitted.

"Sorry."

"Don't be. It was flattering, even when it was embarrassing."

"I never meant to embarrass you. I promise," she added solemnly, "it'll never happen again."

One corner of his mouth twitched. "Too bad. Now I might appreciate it more."

He turned on his heel and walked on before she could respond to that. So Grant McClure still had a wicked sense of humor, she thought. Because he had been joking. He had to have been.

She trotted a few steps to catch up with him. He didn't slow to accommodate her shorter strides, but she was used to that, and just walked faster to keep up. It helped keep her in shape, she reasoned, which was a good thing, no matter how annoying it might be.

"So Chipper just started working here?"

"Year-round, yes. He worked summers before, and used to come out on weekends, with his mother."

His mother? Mercy thought. "Oh?" was all she said.

"Rita does some cooking for us."

Rita. An image of a dark, flashing-eyed brunette passed thorough her mind, and she couldn't stop herself doing the math. Chipper was eighteen; if his mother had married young, she could be as young as thirty-six now. Only six years older than Grant. Hardly a prohibitive difference.

She hoped Chipper's father was big and burly and cranky, then chastised herself for the thought. What did it matter to her, anyway?

"She only cooks on weekends?" she said brightly.

"Yes, but she cooks up a storm. Enough for the whole week, and we freeze it. And she taught a couple of us enough to get through the winter when we run out of her stuff.''

"Sounds like a good plan to me," she said.

"The cooking in advance, or teaching us to cook?"

"Both," she said with a laugh. "I'm not much of a cook myself, as Kristina can tell you."

"She already did. Right after she informed me of how politically incorrect it would be of me to assume that because you're female, you would cook."

"Well," Mercy said in exaggerated relief, "I'm glad that's out of the way."

"I'm sure her warning saved me from a horrible fate."

"Assuredly," Mercy agreed in mock seriousness. "But I do a fine job washing dishes. Perhaps that talent might be of some use?"

"Take it up with the guys. They usually draw straws."

"They? Not you?"

He grinned. "There are some perks to being the boss."

She was still smiling back at him, and marveling at this unexpected lightheartedness that seemed to have overtaken her, when a trumpeting neigh snapped her head around. She turned to stare at the animal who stood in the large corral beside the biggest of the two barns she could see.

The phrase that popped into her head was *flash and fire*, because this animal certainly seemed to have both. He was spectacularly marked. His head, neck and forequarters—she thought that was the right term on a horse—were a glistening black. From the shoulders, or whatever they were—she knew that wasn't right—back over his rump and halfway down his legs, he was a pristine white with scattered dark oval spots that ranged from speckles to almost four inches across.

Something tugged at the edges of her memory. When she was so infatuated with the teenage Grant McClure, and with all the industriousness of a young girl in the throes of her first crush, she'd determined to learn all about the things Grant was so enamored of and she knew nothing about. So she'd read, endlessly, it had seemed, about horses. And although she'd never gotten close to a real one before, beyond driving past some in a pasture somewhere, a lot of that had stuck in her mind. Not the word for shoulders, but a picture of a horse marked like this one, although brown and white, instead of black.

"An...Appaloosa?" she asked, trying the word out tentatively as she walked toward the fence.

"Yes," Grant said, sounding surprised. "He's an Appy."

"I saw a picture of one once," she said, keeping it vague; never would she have admitted the lengths the child she'd been had gone to to learn about what he cared about. "Only it was brown and white."

"They come in all colors. And some are all white, with the spots. Leopard Appies, they call them. I've got a leopard mare who's in foal to him," he said, nodding toward the big horse.

She came to a halt, staring at the animal who towered over her. But she wasn't afraid of him, especially when he cocked his head to look at her with every evidence of interest.

"He's...beautiful." The horse snorted as if he'd

understood, tilting his big head as if preening. Mercy laughed.

"He's a direct descendent of Chief of Four Mile, a premier Appaloosa stud in Texas thirty, forty years ago. But don't let the fancy lineage fool you. He's a clown," Grant said dryly.

"I can see that," she agreed. "And that spot over his eye makes him look like one."

It was true, she thought, that odd-looking white patch over one eye gave the horse a slightly off-center look that was comical despite his size and obvious power.

"Careful," Grant said as she leaned on the top rail of the fence. "He may look and act like a clown, but he's a stallion, and they can be unpredictable."

She backed up a half step. "You mean like biting and kicking? He does that?"

"Well…no. At least he hasn't yet."

"Oh. So you haven't had him very long?"

"A little over a year and a half."

She blinked. "He hasn't kicked or bitten anyone in all that time, but you're still worried?"

Grant looked a little sheepish. "I'm not worried, I'm…baffled. I've never known a stallion who didn't have at least one bad habit."

"And he doesn't?"

"Not unless you count knocking my hat off every time I get close enough," he said wryly.

Mercy chuckled, and the sound was quickly echoed by a soft whicker from the big horse. It was as if he'd had enough of being ignored. She glanced at Grant, who lifted a shoulder in a half shrug.

"You'll be okay. He really does have excellent

manners. Just don't make sudden moves that might startle him. Or touch him before he invites it.''

He didn't explain, so Mercy assumed it would be clear to her if and when that happened. She took back the half step she'd surrendered at Grant's warning. The horse stretched his nose over the fence toward her, nostrils flaring as he sniffed. She let him. His breath stirred her hair, and then, amazingly, she felt the soft touch of his velvety muzzle as he snuffled her ponytail.

The horse whickered again. He nudged the side of her head with his nose, then drew back, as if expectant. He repeated the action after a moment when she didn't move, and Mercy felt like a not-too-intelligent creature the big Appy was trying to train. Was this the invitation Grant had meant?

She glanced at him; he was watching intently, but his expression was unreadable, and he gave her no clue. Was he testing her somehow, for some reason of his own? And if she failed, would she be banished to the house for the duration of her stay?

You, she told herself, *are paranoid.*

And with a smile she reached up very slowly, very carefully, and patted the sleek black neck. The whicker came again, only this time Mercy would have sworn it held a note of pleasure—whether at her touch or at the fact that she'd finally figured it out, she wasn't sure.

"Does he have a name?" she asked, marveling at the muscle and heat and glossiness of the animal.

"I call him Joker."

She chuckled as she looked over her shoulder at Grant; she was almost getting used to laughing again.

"I can see why," she said. "But is that really his name? You said you *call* him Joker."

"His registered name is Fortune's Fire."

Mercy's eyes widened. "Fortune? As in the Fortunes?"

He nodded. "Kate left him to me."

"Kristina's grandmother? Who died in that plane crash?"

He nodded again. An odd expression came over his face as Mercy watched, one of bemusement, even bewilderment.

"He's worth…more than this whole place, probably, when it comes down to it," Grant said. "And I have no idea why she did it."

That was the reason for that expression, she thought. He truly didn't know why Kate Fortune had left him this beautiful animal. It wasn't the animal himself that had him bemused, it was the fact that he owned it. She turned to look at him steadily.

"Well, your mother married her son, right?" she said. "So you were her son Nate's stepson. Her grandson, in a way."

"I suppose." He sounded as puzzled as he looked. "But *I* wasn't really anything to *her*. I'm not a Fortune. I never have been. Not that they haven't been…nice enough, and I know Mom's been married to Nate for twenty-five years, but…I just don't fit in that family."

"Kate obviously thought you did, if she left you such a valuable animal."

He shook his head. "I still don't get it. She left that ranch to my stepbrother Kyle, and Joker should have gone with it. If Kyle had known more about stock, I'm sure he would have fought it. He should have.''

"Since he didn't know, maybe he didn't care."

"I tried to tell him how much the horse was worth, that there was no reason for Kate to leave him to me—"

"You tried to give back what Kate wanted you to have, because you didn't think you should have it?"

Mercy felt an odd tightness in her chest as she remembered Grant at seventeen, lamenting rather than celebrating his victory in a high school swim meet, because the opposing team's champion had been ill and unable to compete. It meant nothing, he said, if you didn't do your best against the best. She'd thought him noble then; apparently he'd never lost that uncompromising honesty.

"I've spent a year and a half trying to figure it out. If his offspring are half the horse he is, he could make this ranch rich. But why? I've seen a lot of Nate, but I'd only met Kate a few times."

"I'd say you made an impression."

He shifted his booted feet, as if he were uncomfortable. Then he shoved his hands into the pockets of his jeans. Jeans worn in a way city men paid a bundle for, Mercy thought, but for all that expense, they still didn't manage to look the way Grant did in them. But then, few men would.

"Maybe," he said doubtfully.

"You don't sound happy about it."

"I'm not a Fortune," he repeated, rather adamantly, Mercy thought. "My mother may have married one, but I don't know how to deal with that kind of life. I don't know how my mother puts up with it.''

"Neither do I," Mercy said frankly. "Sometimes I look at Kristina and envy her, with all that wealth and position, but most of the time I'm just grateful it's not me."

Grant's eyes widened slightly. Then he smiled, a wide, companionable smile that she remembered from the days when he'd actually unbent to talk to the twelve-year-old pest who had become his shadow. Even when he was exasperated with her, he'd never been mean or cruel. But she doubted Barbara Fortune would have tolerated such behavior in her son; Kristina's and Grant's mother was the warmest, kindest woman Mercy had ever met. She made Sheila, Nate's first wife, look like exactly what she was, a grasping, manipulative woman who resented losing the status being a Fortune wife had given her.

"So am I," Grant agreed fervently. "The Fortunes may be as close to royalty as this country gets, but I wouldn't want their problems. I always figured they were a living example of why the Minnesota state bird is the common loon."

Mercy blinked, then laughed. Grant's wry commonsense outlook, which he'd had even as a teenager, was exactly what she needed, she thought.

"That much money does strange things to people," she said.

"And the people around them."

Mercy remembered the night Kristina, devastated by the death of her grandmother, had poured out the long, convoluted and dramatic history of her family.

"Yes," she said, quietly now. "It must have hurt Kate Fortune terribly when her baby was kidnapped."

Grant's expression turned solemn. "My mother

told me Kate never believed the baby was dead. She never gave up, because they never found a body.''

Mercy shivered. "How awful. But Kristina says her aunt Rebecca is just as stubborn. She's convinced the crash that killed Kate was no accident, even after all this time.''

Grant's mouth twisted wryly. "That's what I mean. When you're part of that kind of family, that kind of thinking comes naturally.''

"I suppose it has to. Things always seem to *happen* to the Fortunes. Look at the Monica Malone case—''

Mercy broke off suddenly, realizing she'd been about to mention what might be a painful subject; Grant might say he wasn't a Fortune, but still…

"You mean Jake?" he asked, meeting her gaze levelly.

"I'm sorry. I shouldn't have said anything.''

"It's all over the front pages. Why shouldn't you?''

"Because he's related to you. Sort of.''

Grant shrugged. "Jake may be my uncle by marriage, but that doesn't mean I have any illusions about him. I've always thought he had a side he didn't show much. He rules the Fortune clan, but sometimes I don't think they really…see him.''

"I find him rather intimidatingly aristocratic," Mercy said honestly. "Maybe you see him more clearly because you're a step removed.''

He looked at her consideringly. "You're a cop— what do you think?''

"I don't know enough about the case to form an opinion. And the lid is on this one, tight. Not even many rumors flying. Money can buy silence, it seems.''

"That doesn't surprise me."

"Did Jake being charged surprise you?"

"Judging from the evidence they found? No. But even so, I find it hard to believe."

"That's only natural. No one wants to believe that about someone you know, or are related to, no matter how distantly."

"I don't know," Grant said wryly. "Somehow it seems to be just the kind of thing to happen in the Fortune family. Those are troubled waters."

Mercy couldn't argue with that. But she had to agree that it was hard to believe that handsome, well-bred, cool, calm Jake Fortune was guilty of the spectacular murder of a Hollywood icon.

But she knew better than most that troubled waters could hide a multitude of sins.

Three

"**H**ey!"

It came out as a yelp, and Grant couldn't help laughing as Joker again tugged Mercy's tidy ponytail into complete disarray. She backed away and gave the big Appy a disgusted look.

"I've got to stop using that apple shampoo," Mercy muttered, tugging at her pale blond hair.

"It's more than that," he said, still chuckling. "I feed him the real thing, and I sure don't get this kind of reaction."

It was nothing less than the truth; in the week she'd been here, Mercy had become the focus of the horse's world. He neighed loudly whenever she came into sight, sulked grumpily if she didn't pay him enough attention, and complained noisily if she paid too much attention to any other horse.

"I'm just somebody new," she said. "Whose hair happens to smell like his favorite snack."

"Not just somebody new, some*thing*. Not many women come here, and those that do tend to stay away from him."

"Ah," Mercy said, smiling again. "So he likes the ladies, is that it?"

"It's part of his job. He is a stallion, after all,"

Grant pointed out, wondering if she would be embarrassed by the earthy explanation.

Mercy's smile became a grin, and Grant realized she wasn't easily embarrassed now, any more than she had been twelve years ago.

"I suppose it is," she said easily. "Maybe you should get him a lady of his own."

"He has a string of them, every breeding season," Grant said dryly.

"A job most males would envy," she said.

He raised a brow at her; had there been a note of sourness in her voice? Almost of accusation? He'd never been one to accept universal guilt for the wrongs done by the entire male population, considerable though they might be, and he wasn't going to start now.

"Maybe," he said. "But the rest might feel sorry for him for being a sucker for a city girl."

Her brows furrowed, and he saw the same expression cross her face that he imagined had just crossed his own, as if she were wondering if he was accusing her of something. He hadn't meant to; he was long past his old anger at city women and the games they played.

"And that's a bad thing?"

"Let's just say city girls belong in the city."

Her brows rose. "I see. And your mother? Does she belong there, too?"

He grimaced at her painfully accurate thrust. Mercy had never been one to back down from a confrontation, and he should have guessed that wouldn't have changed. Especially since she was now a cop.

"She feels she belongs with Nate. Wherever that

might be. But she's happy, and that's all that matters."

"But you'd rather she was happy back here."

Grant let out a short breath, sorry he'd ever started this. "What I'd rather doesn't matter, either. Even though she was born here in Wyoming, she felt...too isolated here. There were no other women on the ranch, the closest neighbor is miles away, and Clear Springs even farther."

"I can understand that," Mercy said, all the challenge vanishing from her voice. "Your mother is a very outgoing, gregarious woman, she likes people, and it would be hard for her to feel so alone."

"Yes."

"Still, it must have been awfully painful for her to leave you here while she moved to Minneapolis. I know how much she loves you. Family is everything to her."

"She didn't leave me. I chose to stay here."

She gave him an odd look that he couldn't quite interpret. "I know. She told me that even at four years old you were a stubborn cowboy."

He drew back a little, and his brows lowered. "My mother told you that?"

"She said when she married Nate she asked if you wanted to come live with them. Your answer was to kick Nate in the shin and run away."

Grant felt himself flush. "My mother talks too much."

"Are you upset because she said it, or because she said it to me?"

"Both," he muttered. But a sudden thought made

his eyes narrow as he looked at her. "Just when did this conversation take place?"

"Oh, right before Christmas, as I recall. I remember helping Kristina with that marvelous tree."

Christmas? Almost a year ago? What had Mercy been doing discussing him with his mother then? And then another thought hit him. He'd been with his family at Christmas last year, and Mercy hadn't even been mentioned, he knew that, or he wouldn't have been so surprised when Kristina called about her. And if she'd been around, he was sure his mother would have mentioned it; she felt it was her duty to try and make Grant feel part of the family, which included telling him about everyone's doings, and that would have included Kristina's closest friend, if she'd been there.

"I was at mom's the whole holiday week last year, and you weren't around," he said.

She'd been off with her now deceased partner and lover, no doubt, Grant thought suddenly, wishing he hadn't said anything. But she didn't react with pain or shock or grief, she merely grinned at him.

"I meant Christmas twelve years ago, Grant."

He blinked. "Oh." Then he scowled at her. "You set me up for that."

"Yep," she agreed blandly. "And you bit."

She turned back to Joker. She patted his neck, then rubbed gently at his velvety nose, and the stallion nickered softly and let out a gusty sigh of unmistakable pleasure. And Grant had to laugh once more.

He'd wondered how she managed to be a cop, as small and delicate and fragile as she seemed. But he was beginning to see that her sense of humor, her wit and her quick intelligence probably went a long way toward making up for whatever she lacked in size, muscle and brawn. She might not be able to physically intimidate, but he had a feeling the person who tried to outwit her or outthink her would quickly learn a sad lesson, and probably wind up outwitted himself.

"Yes, you big lunk," she said to the horse, in a soft tone that proved she wasn't at all immune to the big Appy's whimsical charm, "you are a beauty. But you know that, don't you? Pretty full of yourself, aren't you?"

Joker snorted, and stretched his neck out for more of her rubbing caresses. Grant watched her small, slender hands stroke the glossy black hide, and felt an odd tightening low in his belly.

"You could make even a city girl like me want to learn to ride, couldn't you?"

Grant looked at her sharply, wondering if her use of his mocking term was meant for him. But she didn't look at him, merely continued her stroking of the blissfully happy horse's heavily muscled neck.

For the first time in his life, Grant McClure found himself envying a horse. And he didn't like the realization one bit.

"Thanks for fixing that bridle for me, Chipper."

The young hand looked at him, startled. "I didn't, Mr. McClure. I didn't have time to get to it, by the time we found that stray colt and I got that fence repaired."

The colt, one of the first of Joker's get that had been born on the M Double C, had gotten out of a small corral on the far side of the brood-mare barn when a top rail gave way and he jumped the remaining two. Not an inconsiderable feat for a yearling. Maybe they had a competitive jumper on their hands, he thought with an inward grin; he'd like to see the stir a flashily colored Appy would make on the Grand Prix circuit.

But what Chipper had said made his forehead crease. "Then when did you sort out that mess in the tack room?"

"Er...I didn't get to that, either. Charlie and I got back so late, really, and I was checking on that leopard mare, you know she's been acting odd—"

Grant held up a hand. "Easy. I wasn't criticizing. I didn't expect you to round up that colt and get back much before dark. But if you didn't clean it up, who did?"

"Probably the same elf who brought in all that wood yesterday, when it was supposed to be my turn."

Grant looked over his shoulder at Walt Masters, a wiry, grizzled older man who had been at the M Double C for decades, who had seen it grow from the small place it had been when Grant's father, Hank McClure, started it to the sprawling, relatively successful spread it was now. He'd been the one to suggest adding blooded performance horses to the ranch's production, citing the tenuous prices for beef in a changing market these days. Grant had been doubtful, then had warmed to the idea, and now the horses were his favorite part of the operation, and, with the addition of Joker, on their way to being the most profitable.

"Not to mention," Walt went on, "refilling the

wood box in the bunkhouse for us poor, mistreated cowboys."

Grant snorted and took a swipe at Walt with his hat. "Mistreated, hell," he said. "You name me one other ranch in the state where the bunkhouse has a pool table and a hot tub for your aching back, you old coot."

The man grinned. "Your pa's probably still twirlin' in his grave over that tub."

Grant smiled. "Probably, Walt. Probably."

He was proud that he was able to say it without wavering. It had taken him a long time to get to the point of accepting his father's too-early death as a topic of conversation. For a long time, he hadn't been able to talk about it at all. But now he took Walt's gentle, affectionate joking in stride, knowing the old man had loved Hank McClure like a brother.

But that didn't mean he cared to dwell on it, and he excused himself and left the barn.

Probably the same elf who brought in all that wood...

Who was, no doubt, the same elf who had mysteriously repaired the rip in the living room curtains, with neat, tidy stitches that were far beyond his own needlework talents, which began and ended with sewing on buttons.

He stepped into the house and closed the door behind him. The air carried the feel of snow, and he guessed it wouldn't be much longer—a week, maybe two—before Wyoming donned its winter coat once more.

He took two steps into the house and then stopped dead. He sniffed, knowing he should recognize the aroma permeating the air, but unable to quite pin it down. Then it hit him; it wasn't one but two distinct smells; the oddly sweet odor of gun-cleaning fluid and, impossibly...bread. Baking bread. His stomach leaped to attention, and told him about it with a fervent growl.

The bread smell made him curious—and hungry—but the gun-cleaning smell made him wary. He headed in that direction first, into the wood-paneled den where his father's collection of weapons was kept, along with his own shotgun and two hunting rifles. The characteristic smell became stronger, although his stomach seemed to prefer concentrating on the appetizing sent of the bread.

He found Mercy in the den, with his Remington .306 laid out on the table beside the gun cabinet. He'd planned to clean it tonight, after using it yesterday to take down the injured deer he'd tracked high into the back country, putting the animal, which had somehow broken a leg, out of its misery. He hadn't really had the time to spare, but neither had he been able to stand the thought of the big-eyed doe struggling along in pain before she inevitably fell victim to some predator a step up on the food chain. He rarely interfered with nature's plan, but something about the way the frightened, agonized deer looked at him had stirred him to help.

He paused in the doorway, watching as Mercy cleaned the weapon with swift, practiced movements. It brought home to him as nothing had yet that this was a woman familiar with weapons, though more often the kind used mostly to control the worst of the world's predators, the two-legged kind. And again the incongruity of it struck him; he tried to picture her dealing with some big, brawny, rowdy drunk. Or some recalcitrant thief or burglar. And the only way he could reconcile it was to think of how she had charmed Joker, and figure she probably did her job the same way, using wit and charm and intelligence, rather than brute strength or force.

She finished, and began to put away the cleaning kit. Grant stepped into the room.

"Want to check it?"

She didn't look at him as she spoke, and he realized she'd known he was there all along.

"No," he said. "It's obvious you know what you're doing."

"Thank you." She gestured toward the rack on the wall beside the cabinet. "It goes there, I presume?"

"Yes."

She made no move to pick up the weapon. "That's up to you, then. I couldn't reach it without climbing all over your couch."

He'd never thought about how high that rack was before. His father had been even taller than he was, his mother five-seven, so he'd never even thought about it. And this simple realization made him marvel yet again that she had managed to do what she had.

He was putting the Remington back on the rack when his stomach reminded him noisily of the other smell saturating the air. A little embarrassed, he finished racking the rifle, then glanced at her. She was grinning.

"It does have that effect, doesn't it?"

"I thought you didn't cook."

"I don't. But I can bake up a storm. I hope you don't mind me invading your kitchen."

"Not," he said fervently, "when the results smell like that. I'm going to have a riot on my hands if that smell gets out."

"I made three loaves. I hope that's enough for everybody."

"When did you have time, between all your other little jobs?"

She didn't deny his words, only shrugged. "I had all day."

"I thought you came here to...recuperate."

That shadow he'd seen before darkened her expression for a moment. But she said only "I can't just sit around. I feel better if I'm doing something."

He couldn't argue with that. Keeping busy was the only thing that had gotten him through the days after his father died. And he'd done it well, kept so busy that he dropped into an exhausted sleep at night. That hadn't stopped the dreams, but on the better days, he hadn't remembered most of them by morning. And eventually they had faded, leaving behind only a lingering sadness, and gradually allowing the good memories to return.

He wondered when Mercy would be able to face Corelli's death without that shadow darkening her eyes.

A couple of nights later, when he found himself with that rarest of things, time on his hands, when he found himself actually considering sitting down with a book, he had to admit that it was because of Mercy, because of all the myriad things she had seen needed doing and had done, the tiny little tasks that he always had to put off until after a full day of ranch work, the things that ate up his evenings until he had no time left for one of the few great pleasures in his life.

He let out a long sigh of satisfaction as he lowered himself into his father's leather recliner and put the footrest up. For a few minutes he just sat there, book in hand, savoring the prospect of peacefully reading for a couple of hours. His eyes drifted closed, and he wondered where Mercy was. She'd been out flirting with Joker when he rode in, but he hadn't seen her since. Nor had she been in the house after he finished his shower; an even lengthier than usual affair after he'd rescued that calf from a mud hole on the south flats. He'd wound up even muddier than the bawling creature, and the mud had dried to a skin-pulling crust by the time he got back to the house.

He opened his eyes suddenly, aware that something had changed. The room was dark, and he thought groggily that the light over the chair had burned out. Then he realized he was swathed in something, and it took him a moment to realize it was the blanket from the back of the couch. He freed one arm and reached out to try the lamp. It came on cooperatively, lighting the chairside table, and his book, neatly closed and sitting beside the lamp.

And the clock on the desk across the room said 3:00 a.m.

Walt? he wondered. No, the old man might have turned out the light, might even, in a fit of helpfulness, have put away his book, but tucking a blanket around him was hardly old Walt's style. And it was unlikely he'd have come back to the house after retiring to the warmth and comfort of the bunkhouse, anyway.

He knew who had probably done it, he just didn't want to admit that Mercy had found him sound asleep and tucked him in like a kid. Didn't want to admit he found it oddly comforting.

He didn't want to admit how much he'd come to like having her around in such a short time.

"She's a tough little thing," Walt said. "Stronger'n she looks, too."

Grant didn't have to ask; even if Walt's words hadn't made it obvious, there was only one "she" on the ranch. Mercy was everything Walt had said, and more.

"She wasn't too happy with me when I tried to help her with that hay bale," Chipper put in rather morosely.

"Did she need help?" Walt asked. Grant had the feeling he already knew the answer.

"Well...no," Chipper admitted, looking sheepish. "She slung that thing on the wagon like she'd been doin' it forever. She is awful strong."

"Learns fast, too," Walt put in. "I had to check on that leopard mare this morning. She's making me nervous with all that pacing around, even though she's not due to foal for another six weeks."

"Me, too," Grant said; the pregnant mare they called simply Lady was one of their most valuable, and she was in foal to Joker. Their first get had been the colt who had escaped the other day, and Grant had hopes this foal might turn out as well. "But what does that have to do with our...visitor?"

"By the time I was done, that girl had all the stalls on this side of the barn shoveled out."

Grant stared at him. "She was mucking out stalls?"

"And doin' a fine job of it, too."

Fixing tack. Stacking wood. Cleaning the tack room. Cleaning his rifle. Baking bread. And now slinging hay bales and cleaning stalls.

She needs to rest, she's running herself ragged.

Kristina's words echoed in his head. If this was what Mercy considered resting, he didn't want to know what she thought was work. And what she'd been doing wasn't just work, it was labor, simple, hard, physical labor, requiring a strength and endurance he never would have guessed she had, from her appearance.

Which should teach him something, he supposed. But he still felt a niggling sense of guilt, as if somehow he'd made her feel she had to earn her keep here, because of his warnings about this being the worst time of year for them here at the ranch. It was true that, while calving time was hectic, and the roundup and branding season was busy, winter was dangerous, to man and beast. But maybe he'd sounded a little harsh to her.

"—goin' to do, son?"

Grant blinked at Walt. "What did you say? I...was thinking."

Walt clucked at him mockingly. "Been doin' a lot o'that lately, boy. Too much thinking ain't good for a man, you know."

"Right," Grant muttered, and turned on his heel and strode out of the barn without another word.

He found Mercy in the house, adding a small log to the fire in the stove. She'd apparently gotten into the habit of replacing what they burned every day, something he had always meant to do but had been unable to, with all the demands on his time; the inside stack hadn't diminished at all since she'd been here.

"You don't have to do all this, you know."

When Mercy straightened and gave him a puzzled look, he knew it had came out rather abruptly, not at all how he'd meant to say it.

"Keep the fire going? It's strictly selfish. I hate it when my teeth chatter indoors."

"That's not what I meant."

She closed the tempered-glass door of the stove, dusted her hands off on her jeans—jeans that hugged her hips and backside delightfully; it didn't seem right that such a little thing had such luscious curves—and turned to face him straight on. A trait he was coming to expect from her. And to suspect was how she faced most things in life.

Except, perhaps, the death of Nick Corelli.

"What did you mean, then?"

"I told you I don't expect you to work."

"And I told you I need to keep busy."

"Fine. Keep busy. What you've been doing is a big help. But you don't have to lug hay bales or clean out stalls."

"I know I don't *have* to."

"That's hard, dirty work. Leave it to the guys whose job it is."

She gave him a calculating look. "Oh. But I suppose baking bread and sewing is all right?"

He'd known when he started this that somehow he was going to end up in trouble.

"I didn't mean that. At least not like that."

"Then just how did you mean it? You think I can't do that kind of work?"

"That would be pretty silly of me, wouldn't it, when you've already proven you can?" he said, trying to be reasonable.

"Then why are you telling me to stop?"

He let out a compressed breath. "I'm not. But you're supposed to be here to rest, not work yourself to death."

"Did you ever stop to think," she said, her voice tight, "that maybe that's the only way I *can* rest?"

"Yes," he said honestly. "Because I've been there. But I'm used to this kind of work. You're not. And even though you're a heck of a lot tougher than you look, you could still get hurt."

She seemed taken aback at his first words, but by the time he finished, that rebellious look was back in her eyes.

"All this macho protective stuff might have been appealing when I was twelve and thought the sun rose and set on you," she snapped, "but I'm not a child anymore, Grant. I don't need protecting."

Grant drew back slightly, both startled and amused by her vehemence. No, it wasn't a child who was standing toe-to-toe with him, facing him down. It was a woman, and a fierce, passionate one, at that.

Unfortunate choice of words, he thought as his body surged in response to thoughts brought on just by thinking the word *passionate* in conjunction with Mercy. Would this ardent intensity carry over into other aspects in her personality? Did she exhibit the same fire and passion in other places, other ways?

If so, he thought wryly as he tried to quell the heat that was suddenly billowing through him, Nick Corelli had been a very lucky man.

And realizing he'd just called a man who had been shot to death on a dirty city street lucky was just the absurdity he needed to rein in his own unexpected and unwanted reaction to this woman he'd spent so much time trying not to think about lately.

"Okay," he said, keeping his voice light with an effort. "I'm just afraid Kristina's going to have my head if she finds out I've been working you so hard."

She accepted the change gracefully. "So that's it—you're afraid of your little sister."

"Any man in his right mind would be afraid of Kristina."

"You're right." Mercy smiled, then sighed. "I always wanted to be like her."

Grant's brows furrowed. "What?"

"You know, glamorous, charming, bubbly. All the things I'm not."

"You'll do just fine as you are," he said gruffly. "The last thing the world needs is another pampered charmer like Kristina. You're solid, steady, and not a bit spoiled."

"Oh, thank you," Mercy said, her mouth twisting wryly. "Just what a girl wants to hear."

She left him standing there gaping after her as she turned and trotted up the stairs.

Women, Grant thought, wondering what the hell he'd said wrong now.

He should, he mused rather sourly, leave the females to Joker.

Four

Mercy stretched, then retreated into the warmth of her curled-up shape when her toes found nothing but cold sheets. She opened her eyes to dim gray light, and sleepily wondered what time it was. A few minutes passed before she decided she cared enough to look at the bedside clock; she hadn't been sleeping well for a long time, and was hesitant to end last night's relatively peaceful rest.

When she saw the clock read past 8:00 a.m., she came awake in a rush; she hadn't slept this late in months. She sat up, rubbing her arms against the room's chill, realizing now that the fire had probably died down to embers, if Grant had been up and out before dawn, as usual. She'd have to hurry downstairs and stoke it before it died out altogether.

She yawned as she scrambled into her jeans and a heavy dark green sweater, then pulled on the sheep-skin boots that were the only thing she'd ever found that kept her feet warm no matter what. And yawned again. No wonder the man fell asleep in his chair, she thought. She hadn't been at all surprised when she found him there that night.

What had surprised her was the book she found resting across his broad chest. Somehow she hadn't expected the rugged cowboy who ramrodded this big ranch to be prone to reading Shakespeare. But there was no doubt he'd been doing just that—the collected tragedies, to be exact. She'd glanced at the shelves behind the sleeping man, and seen more Shakespeare, Molière and a few more classics tucked in among a selection of much more recent technothrillers, reminding her that Grant had been torn between majoring in literature and studying engineering, despite his never-wavering determination to return to the ranch.

Then she realized she shouldn't have been surprised. She'd known perfectly well that Grant had graduated college with honors; Kristina had told her so, proud of her big brother's success. She remembered when he'd left for college that last summer when she was fourteen. She'd wept, certain her white knight was leaving forever and she'd never see him again. And then she'd started high school herself, and by the following summer she'd been far too sophisticated to spend her time mooning over a childhood crush.

But that hadn't stopped her that night from simply standing beside the worn leather chair, watching Grant McClure sleep. The mouth that was so mobile, as quick to smile as it was to frown or quirk in wry amusement, had looked warm and relaxed, and the sandy brown semicircles of his lashes had looked thick and soft against his tanned cheeks. Free for the moment of the responsibility of keeping this ranch going, he had looked much as he had when she last saw him, eighteen and off to conquer the world.

And her world hadn't ended, as she'd feared it would. No, she'd left her childhood passion far behind. No longer was her singular goal in life to snag Grant McClure's attention. And the fact that when he joked that he might appreciate her attention now her heart had taken a sudden leap, and a burst of heat had shot through her, was something she would just as soon ignore. It reminded her far too much of the infatuated child she'd been.

She yawned again, and stretched as she went down the stairs. Still sleepy-eyed, she stirred the coals in the stove until they were glowing brightly, then added three small, dry pieces of kindling. They caught quickly, and she added two larger pieces of wood. When they were burning, too, she shut the stove door. She stood there for a few minutes, until the heat began to radiate again, warming her hands at the rekindled fire.

Somewhat absently, still pondering the near miracle of her almost restful night's sleep, she wandered over to the front window and lifted the curtain she'd mended last week. And blinked.

Snow. Everything was covered with it. As if all color had been wiped from the earth's palette, revealing a spotless canvas.

She'd always welcomed the first snow back in the city. The pristine white cloak seemed to mask, even if only for a while, the ugliness she too often encountered in her work. She knew it was only a facade, that all the ugliness was still there, but it lightened the load just a little to pretend for a short time that the world was as clean and bright as it looked after that first snow. But here the landscape itself had its own clean, stark beauty, and the coating of snow softened it all to a gentle loveliness.

She went for her heavy shearling coat and pulled it on, then trotted to the door. The moment she stepped outside, she took in a long, deep breath of crisp air that seemed so clean she could almost taste the purity of it. She found herself smiling, and her smile widened as she stepped off the porch into the pure white and heard it crunch under her feet.

She grinned widely to herself.

And then she stopped dead, marveling. She'd been doubtful when Kristina suggested this; going to a quiet place with nothing to do but think hadn't seemed to her a wise thing to do. Even though she'd thought seeing Grant after all these years, and seeing how her childhood hero had turned out, might be an interesting distraction, she hadn't thought it would be enough to get her mind off Nick. And the fact that more than anything, she knew, she should be back home, hunting down the men who had killed him.

But she'd underestimated. Grant McClure was enough to take anyone's mind off their problems. Of course, that also presented a whole new set of problems, but she thought she'd be able to chide herself out of her own silly reaction to the man. It was just some leftover trace of her childish infatuation, that was all. And, she admitted with an inward smile, proof that even as a child she'd had good taste. Grant was as good-looking now as he had been at sixteen, when she first laid eyes on him. Better, in fact. He'd done more than age gracefully, he'd done it beautifully; at thirty, he was...

Words failed her. That was something that was rare enough that her inward smile turned rueful. Grant had always had that effect on her. That fact had never bothered her back then. But now, now that she was an adult and supposedly immune to such things, she found it irritating, and she chastised herself seriously and with more than a little chagrin. The man had made it more than clear that she wasn't his type. *You're solid, steady, and not a bit spoiled.* Delightful, she thought. He could have been talking about a dog. Or a horse.

Her mouth quirked. Well, maybe not a horse. Judging from Grant's assessment of her charms, she apparently had considerably less personal appeal than the fiery and flashy Joker. So why didn't she take the hint and quash these stupid, juvenile feelings she was having?

Maybe she was doing it on purpose, she thought suddenly. Perhaps some defensive part of her mind was busy making Grant the only distraction powerful enough to divert her thoughts from the memories that haunted her. The mind acted in strange ways to protect itself; she'd seen vivid evidence of that more than once.

So was she only imagining the way her heart sped up when she saw him, or the wave of tenderness that had swept over her as she watched the man who worked so hard asleep in a chair, a volume of Shakespeare in strong hands toughened by ranch work? She didn't think so. But—

"Testing how long it will take you to freeze just standing there?"

She whirled around at the sound of Grant's voice, wondering how on earth he'd snuck up on her again. Usually she was very much aware of her surroundings and any movement in them; it was a necessary by-product of her work.

"I...love the first snow," she said, hoping the flush rising to her cheeks looked like merely a reaction to the cold.

"This isn't like the city. No snowplows come and clear a path for you. The novelty will wear off when we're under six feet of it and you can't get out for days."

She studied him for a moment. "You seem compelled to continually point out that I live in the city. Do you think I've forgotten?"

He lifted one shoulder in a shrug that might have meant anything. "Just a reminder."

A reminder for who? she wondered. But as she retreated to the shelter of the covered porch, she said only, "That I'm a city girl? I'm hardly likely to forget that."

"City girls never do." Grant followed her up the two wooden steps, then turned to look out over the whitened landscape. "They might like to visit a remote place like this, for a while, when it's warm and sunny and the new calves and foals are frolicking around, but they can't handle living here."

Kristina, Mercy thought. She'd said almost exactly that. *Grant lives and breathes that ranch,* she'd said. *And I'll admit it's beautiful, in a desolate sort of way, and the baby animals are precious, but give me city lights.*

"Kristina..." she began, then stopped, not sure she should venture into this territory, half-afraid it was going to come back on her.

Grant gave that half shrug again, just a lifting of

his right shoulder beneath his heavy jacket. "She might not be as spoiled as she is if she'd had to live here for a while, away from the bright lights and phony glitter. But she's a city girl born and bred, and she'll never change."

"Maybe you need a reminder," she said quietly. "I'm not Kristina." Or your mother, she added, but silently, doubting very much that he needed or wanted that pointed out to him.

"No, you're not," he agreed easily enough. "But you're a city girl, as well."

"Once a city girl, always a city girl, is that it?" She was beginning to feel a bit testy about his assumptions, although she was beginning to see why he had this particular blind spot.

"It would be tough to change," he said, with as much of an effort at diplomacy as she'd ever seen from him on the subject. "I couldn't learn to live in the city, either. I've always known that."

"Since you were four?"

He smiled, but it wasn't a particularly happy one. "Before that, even. This is my home. It always has been, and it always will be."

Mercy sat on the wide porch swing that added an unexpectedly homey touch to the utilitarian house; made of carved cedar, it was a beautiful piece.

"My father bought that for Mom for their anniversary," Grant said. "Had it shipped in from a little shop outside San Antonio. He hoped if she sat there enough, she would learn to see the beauty here. She did see it, but it wasn't enough. Or it was already too late. She'd already made up her mind to leave."

"So you kicked your stepfather and told your

mother no when she asked you to live with them. Vehemently, I gather.''

"I was only four," Grant said, sounding a bit testy himself. "I wanted my mother and father together again. I suppose I thought if I chose to stay here, she'd eventually come home.''

"But she and Nate were already married.''

"That doesn't make much difference to a four-year-old.'' He grimaced. "But I shouldn't have kicked Nate.''

"He lived," Mercy said wryly. "And he does love your mom.''

"I know. Sometimes I think she's the only person he truly does love. He cares about his kids, but...''

"I know. I've only met Jane and Michael, but they seemed so unsure of how their father feels about them.'' She gave Grant a sideways look. "At least you can't doubt your mother loves you.''

"Not anymore. I wasn't convinced when my little ruse didn't work, but by the time I was ten, I got over it.''

"At least she respected your decision.''

"Yes, she did. She always has. Considering that most people think I'm wasting myself out here, that's quite a concession.''

"Wasting yourself?''

He crossed his arms over his chest, and Mercy wondered what had been said to make him he adopt such a defensive posture even now.

"'You're a smart boy, Grant, you can do something with your life,''' he quoted sourly. "'You've got a degree, Grant, what are you doing out here in the middle of nowhere, nursemaiding cows?' 'Four years of college, gone to waste.'"

Mercy met his gaze and held it levelly. "Is it what you want to do?"

"It's the only thing I've ever wanted to do." He said it with a grim determination that spoke volumes about how many times he'd had to defend his choice.

"Then tell them to mind their own business." He gave her a startled look. "I've seen too many people locked into jobs they hate. I've seen what it does to them, and those around them. If you're happy with your work, then it's right."

He smiled suddenly, warmly. Mercy felt as if the sun had abruptly come out.

"That's what my mother finally told me," he said, "the last time Nate lit into me."

"Good for her. Sometimes I think that's the hardest thing for a parent to do, to respect a decision their child makes that they don't agree with."

Grant leaned against a porch post, giving her a speculative look. "The voice of experience?"

She nodded. "My folks wanted me to be a doctor."

Grant blinked. "A doctor? That's...quite a change, doctor to cop."

"And they weren't happy about it. I had applied and been accepted to a couple of colleges with good medical schools. I knew I wanted to...help people, but I finally realized that wasn't how I wanted to do it." Her mouth twisted into a rueful, mocking smile. "Little did I know."

"Know...what?"

"That half the people I deal with don't *want* to be helped. They just want the police around to pick up the pieces afterward.'' She shivered. ''Some of them even want the cops to solve all their problems permanently. They can't pull the trigger themselves, so they set up a cop to do it for them. Like we were machines, with no feelings at all—''

She broke off abruptly, realizing her voice was rising and her tangled emotions were on the verge of breaking loose.

''I...I'm sorry. I didn't mean to...''

She bit her lip, stopping the broken flow of words. She felt the stinging behind her eyelids, and knew that she'd been blindsided, that talking about one of the most difficult aspects of her job had opened the door for the thoughts about the worst. Her calm since she'd been here was apparently only a facade, not true peace. Another shiver rippled through her, and it had nothing to do with the cold.

Suddenly Grant was beside her on the swing; she hadn't even heard him move. She was too surprised to react when he put his arms around her, and once he had, his solid strength and his radiating warmth were too comforting to pull away from.

''It's an ugly, dangerous job, Mercy,'' he said softly. ''I've always known that, but I'm afraid I never thought much—not enough, anyway—about the people who do it. Until now.''

His obvious concern warmed her, but the inner alarms were going off like mad. In her current state of mind, his strength and warmth was too comforting, too tempting...and far too dangerous.

She drew back from his embrace, trying not to do it as abruptly as she wanted to, just to free herself from the lure of his closeness.

"I'm sorry to have dumped on you," she said, rather stiffly.

He looked at her intently, but didn't protest her movement or answer her words. She stood up and moved away, until there was a relatively safe three feet between them.

"I've been...having lots of second thoughts about my job lately," she said when the silence became too tense for her. "But that doesn't mean you have to listen to my sob story."

"It sounds," Grant said after a moment, "like you need to tell someone."

Not you, Mercy thought instantly; the last thing she needed was to share her darkest thoughts with this man, who was already proving far too unsettling to her tenuous peace of mind.

"I need to work through it myself," she insisted.

"I see you're just as stubborn as you were twelve years ago."

"I'm not stubborn, just because I deal with my problems myself."

"I didn't say not to deal with them yourself. Just to talk about them to somebody. Or would that impinge on your sense of independence?"

She gave him a sharp glance. "I thought men were the ones who thought women talked about things too much."

"Maybe that's it. You work around men too much—you've lost the knack. Or do cops bare their souls to each other?"

Mercy's brows furrowed, until she saw the glint of teasing humor in his bright blue eyes. "Cops," she said wryly, "tend to bottle things up until they explode. Most of them, anyway."

"And you?"

"I won't blow up. I'm not the type, according to the department psychologist."

"You went to a psychologist?"

"It's S.O.P., after...a shooting."

"Did it...help?"

"Some." She glanced out at the snow-covered panorama; she was starting to get beyond chilled, sitting out here, not moving. "He thought coming here was a good idea."

"And do you? Now that you've been here a few days?"

"Maybe. It's beautiful, and there's an elemental wildness here that...appeals to me. There's a sort of pureness to it. It's harsh, but...it's clean, not evil. It's just...life."

Grant looked startled at her words. "I... That's...how I've always felt. It's why I know I could never be really happy anywhere else."

For a long, silent moment, they simply looked at each other, blue eyes holding green, both clearly aware of the unexpected bond that had just leaped to life between them.

It was so powerful it almost frightened her; she didn't want to feel this, didn't want to feel anything right now, when she knew, in her mind that she was so very vulnerable. Unfortunately, it was her heart that was reacting, not her head. Still, she knew she had to put some distance between them, even though she knew, as well, that there was no denying what had just happened. So—typically, perhaps—she confronted them instead.

"But there are...distractions I hadn't foreseen," she said.

The look he gave her then made her feel uncomfortably as if he'd read her mind. "Distractions?"

Bad mistake, Brady, she muttered to herself. "Among other things, the fact that I'm going numb," she said. *In the head,* she added to herself, but escaped to the warmth of the house before she could get herself into any more trouble.

Meredith Cecelia Brady was the most...the most... the most maddening woman he'd ever known, just as she'd been the most maddening child.

Grant turned over in bed and yanked the thick down comforter up to his nose, although he wasn't particularly cold. The snow had continued off and on all day and into the night, and the thickness that had built up on the roof acted as another layer of insulation. Despite the slight wind that had kicked up, the house was, if anything, a bit warmer than it was on a snowless winter night.

The people who made the calendars that said winter didn't start until December had never spent much time here, he thought. Winter started whenever it darn well pleased.

The weather wasn't much of a diversion; his thoughts slid right back into the rut they'd been languishing in since the day Mercy had arrived. She'd driven him crazy twelve years ago, and it didn't seem she'd lost the talent for doing it. That it was now an entirely different and vastly more uncomfortable and disturbing kind of crazy only made things worse.

She was even disrupting his sleep, he who generally slept like the dead after a long day's work. But here he was, tossing and turning, hearing slight wind noises he usually slept through, staring at the ceiling, ordering himself not to look at the clock and see how short a time he had left before he would have to roll out and go back to work.

Another creaking sound, seeming annoyingly loud in his cranky mood, made him roll over onto his back in disgust. *You should just get your sorry butt out of bed now, McClure,* he thought. You could have gotten half your day's work done in the time you've been wasting thinking about that woman.

And wondering exactly what other distractions she'd been talking about.

A noise that sounded, impossibly, like the downstairs door opening interrupted his unwelcome contemplations.

Walt, he thought. Maybe something was wrong.

He rolled out, dressing with a haste that wasn't entirely due to the cold. He pulled on his heavy wool socks, but grabbed up his boots to carry them; he might not need to put them on, and he didn't want to wake Mercy clattering down the stairs.

Except, he realized as he stepped out into the hall and headed toward the top of the stairway, she was apparently already awake; the door to the guest room stood wide open. He glanced in as he went past, and saw blankets and the bright blue quilt strewn about in a manner that spoke of a sleep as restless—or as nonexistent—as his own. She must have heard the same thing he had, and come down to investigate.

"Walt?" he called out as he went down the stairs. No answer came back at him, and he traversed the last half-dozen steps at a run. He came into the living room, skidding slightly in sock feet on the wood floor. Then he stopped dead, staring at the front door, which was standing wide open.

Not Walt, he thought. He would never do such a thing, leave the door standing ajar like that, letting all the heat from the wood stove escape. Not when it was snowing like this outside; it was a flurry much thicker than he'd expected to see.

"Mercy?" he called out. Still no answer. Irritated as much as mystified, he strode over to the door that led into the kitchen. The room was dark and quiet. He turned and went back toward the front door, pausing to stuff another log into the stove. He'd shut the damn door, then figure out what had happened. He knew it hadn't blown open—he was too careful for that—and city girl or not, he didn't think Mercy would be so careless either. She might be—

Outside, he realized as, one hand on the doorknob, he stared out at the tracks in the thin layer of soft snow that had accumulated, thanks to the wind, on the porch floor. Small tracks, made by tiny, delicate feet, not his own size elevens, or Walt's extrawides.

What the hell?

He yanked on his boots, grabbed his heavy coat from the rack by the door and a flashlight from the shelf above the rack. Pulling the door shut behind him, he stepped onto the porch. The tracks led to the steps, down them, then straight ahead. Then they veered to the right, toward the main barn.

He went down the steps, wincing when, as he cleared the shelter of the porch, the wind bit into the exposed flesh of his face. It was stronger than he'd thought, and he didn't want to speculate what the temperature was with the windchill factor figured in.

Fury welled up in him. What the hell was she doing, traipsing around out here in the middle of the night, and in the middle of a snow flurry to boot? Didn't she realize how dangerous weather like this could be? Didn't she know that a person could get utterly disoriented in the pure, blowing whiteness, and freeze to death a few feet from safety he never knew was there? How could she be so half-witted? So careless? He'd thought maybe she wasn't quite as city-stupid as he'd feared, but now...

A sense of urgency he'd never known before seized him, and he sped up his pace, straining to see the faint trail, which was growing fainter by the moment as the snow continued to fall. His powerful flashlight wasn't worth much in the thick snow; it reflected back as much as it showed forward.

He lost the trail to the gathering snow twenty yards from the house. He had to guess she'd been headed for the barn; he prayed she'd made it the last forty feet. The sliding door was closed, but not latched, and his tension eased a notch.

And then tightened again in a rush as he slid it open and stepped inside.

And saw Mercy crumpled on the floor outside Joker's stall.

Five

Joker whinnied—a plaintive sound Grant had never heard from the big stallion before. It galvanized him, and he broke into a run. He slid on some loose straw and nearly went down, but recovered and kept going. Joker whinnied again, bobbing his head toward Mercy as he thrust it through the open top half of the stall's Dutch door, as if he were afraid Grant hadn't seen her. Grant barely managed to stop himself from telling the animal he had, as if the stallion would understand.

She was shivering violently, her arms wrapped around herself as if she were trying to hold herself together, or physically hang on to what body heat she had left after her foolish trek through the snow. It was relatively warm here inside the barn, though not as warm as in the house, and that trek across the yard in the blowing snow would have sapped body heat rapidly.

At least some instinctive level of self-preservation had been functioning, Grant thought as he knelt beside her; she'd put on her heavy sheepskin boots and jacket. But what the hell was that she had on underneath? Some flimsy pale green thing, as if she'd run out into the snow in her nightgown or something...

She had done just that, he realized.

"Are you completely crazy?" he snapped, reaching for her.

He pulled her up to a sitting position, and opened his mouth to deliver a scathing rebuke. She looked up at him then, and the moment he saw her eyes, all his anger, all the fierce words that were about to burst loose, faded away.

He'd never seen anyone look so utterly, completely devastated. Her eyes were wide with remembered terror, and he realized her trembling was not from cold but from reaction; she looked like someone being chased by a horror too great to face. Any idea he'd had of scolding her for her foolishness vanished.

"Mercy?" he said, as softly, as gently, as he could. "What is it? What happened?"

Her arms tightened around her, and she rocked back and forth with a tiny moan. And suddenly it didn't matter to him any longer what had happened, what horror had driven her out into the snowy night, risking illness or even death; he had a fairly good idea what it was, anyway.

He pulled open the lower stall door. It was foolish, perhaps, to trust the stallion in such a way, but the animal was so besotted with Mercy, he doubted he would do anything that might hurt her. And the big horse's body heat would be welcome. He lifted Mercy inside, putting her down on the clean straw, closed the door again, then moved to sit beside her, opening his jacket and pulling her to him, tucking her legs, clad only in that thin green fabric he supposed was silk, against his, adding his own heat to what little she had left. That she didn't fight him, didn't pull away, told him more about her state of mind than any words could have.

Joker whickered softly, lowering his nose to snuffle the top of Mercy's head with exquisite care.

"She'll be all right," Grant assured the stallion, not even caring about the absurdity of reassuring the horse; the words were meant for Mercy, just as much as for the big Appy. And probably, he admitted as she continued to shake against him, for himself, as well.

"She just needs to get warm, and know that she's safe, that it's okay," he said, continuing the pretense of comforting the horse. At least he thought it was pretense, but the stallion's soft nickers seemed to change; as if he'd understood, they became gentle rather than plaintive.

It had been a long time since he'd tried to comfort a woman. He wasn't sure he'd been any good at it the few times he tried in the past, and lately he'd avoided getting close enough to one to be called upon to do it, unless it was perhaps Kristina after one of her peccadilloes, or his mother when Nate pulled something she didn't approve of.

And never had he tried to comfort a woman as distraught as this one. Probably because he'd never really known a woman who had to deal with the kind of nightmares Mercy's work no doubt left her with.

For a long time, he just sat there, holding her, trying to assess whether or not her quivering had lessened. She let him press her head to his shoulder, and he found himself dodging Joker's black muzzle as the animal periodically nosed her hair, as if trying to get her to react as she usually did, with mock indignation. She didn't.

He knew now what her hair looked like down; a thick golden mane that felt as silky as it looked. He could detect the faint fragrance of the now infamous apple-scented shampoo, the smell she teasingly swore was the secret of her easy captivation of the horse. But what he detected most of all was the constant shivers that rippled through her.

He was aware that she probably wore little or nothing beneath the nightgown that spilled out from beneath her jacket; the fragile, delicate fabric looked rather odd over the heavy sheepskin boots. He could picture too well how she would look in it, how the pale green shade would light her eyes to the peridot of the ring his mother sometimes wore. He was even aware, on some other level that wasn't intent on simply offering comfort, that his body was responding to her closeness, but he quashed the response mercilessly; it would be the worst kind of insult to make that kind of move now, and bad enough if she was to even guess at his reaction.

And the kind of woman Mercy was, who lived every day with the kind of thing that left her feeling like this, didn't deserve that kind of insult, even if he was capable of dealing it.

So instead he kept talking, not even sure of what he said, just soothing, gentling words, as if he were calming a frightened horse. He held her close, but not tightly; he didn't want her to feel trapped, something he imagined would be far too easy, with their difference in size.

And she let him. She stayed there, huddled against

him, still shaking slightly but otherwise motionless, and utterly silent. At last, when her trembling seemed to have subsided, he lapsed into silence himself, but still held her.

Joker seemed to relax, as well, although he watched Mercy with an alert intensity that made Grant wonder just how much the Appy understood. Animals were sensitive to human moods, he knew that; more than once, when he took Joker out in a rowdy, reckless mood, the animal had seemed to catch it, and welcome a breakneck race across the sagebrush-and-greasewood-dotted flats. And when he was grumpy for one reason or another, the animal had seemed to know it immediately, and had stood looking at him, head tilted at an angle that inevitably made Grant think of the phrase *Get over it!*

He didn't know how long they'd been sitting there before Mercy finally spoke, in a low, small voice, words that sounded forced.

"I'm...sorry."

He didn't speak, just tightened his arms around her for a moment.

"I..."

Her voice trailed off, and he felt her move, moving her head against his shoulder as if to snuggle closer to him. The tiny movement, and the trust it implied, warmed him far beyond what he would ever have expected.

"I thought it was gone. The dream. I hadn't had it...since I came here."

So it was some kind of awful nightmare that had driven her out into the night.

"I'm sorry I made you talk about it this afternoon. Maybe that's what brought on the dream."

"The...doctor said I should talk about it." He heard her sigh, a faint release of her breath that was barely audible. "Like you said. But it's...hard. Everybody I know...knew Nick. They were grieving, too, and it seemed...so wrong to talk to them about what happened, because it was so awful, and I could never tell them the real truth, it was too horrible, too bloody, too ugly, and they were his friends, his family—"

She bit off the tumbling words, and he felt her shiver again. He again tightened his hold, and she didn't fight him—seemed, in fact, to lean into his embrace.

He didn't think he wanted to hear it, didn't want to know what had the power to haunt this strong, resilient woman so completely, but he also knew he couldn't bear to see her hurting so, couldn't stand to see her try to control it so valiantly when it was screaming, clawing, to be let out.

"Tell me," he whispered. "Tell me, Mercy."

"I...can't."

"Yes, you can." Joker nudged her with his nose, as if to encourage her himself. "Who better is there? I didn't know him, it won't hurt me, not like it would them."

"I..."

"What happened, Mercy? Kristina only told me he'd been killed in the line of duty."

"He wasn't just killed. He was...executed."

Now he knew for sure he didn't want to hear this,

but he couldn't back out now, not when she'd begun to talk at last.

"Go on," he prompted, his voice far steadier than he expected.

"We'd been involved…in an ongoing investigation."

Grant sensed she was being purposely vague, but he didn't push; he supposed there were some things cops just didn't talk about to civilians, no matter the circumstances, no matter how distracted or upset they were. The training went too deep. Name, rank and serial number, even under torture; military, yes, but he doubted the principles were much different.

"Nick got a tip, from an informant he'd been working with for a while, on the murder of another officer, a friend, a couple of years ago. He trusted the guy."

Something in her tone gave her away. "But he shouldn't have?"

"The snitch gave him up. And set him up. The guys we were after were waiting for him in that warehouse. It was an ambush from the get-go."

She shuddered once, violently, then again, and Grant instinctively tightened his embrace. He waited silently until the tremors faded, until she was again quiet in his arms. He more than ever didn't want to hear the rest of this, supposed she would stop if he didn't push her, but he also knew she needed to get it out.

"Finish it," he said, a little hoarsely.

"I… No. It doesn't matter. Doesn't change anything."

"Finish it, Mercy."

For a moment, he thought she was going to refuse.

But he felt the capitulation in her posture even before the words came, haltingly, in chunks of sound made up of equal parts pain and rage and guilt.

"They...tied his hands. Behind him. And shot him...in the back of the head."

"Damn."

"He never had a chance. Except me. And I was too late. He was already dying...when I got to him."

Grant went very still; he hadn't known this. "You...were there?"

"I was his partner. Of course I was there." Her voice turned harsh, bitter. "For all the good it did him. He—" She gulped, a jerky little intake of air that he felt, as well as heard. "He was bleeding. So much blood. His head...was..." She shuddered, violently. "He was still breathing. But his eyes...they were already... He died in my arms."

Oh, God, Grant thought. "Mercy—"

"If I'd been a minute sooner. One little minute. If I'd not stopped to call it in, hadn't taken the time to ask for backup, if I'd just gone ahead and followed him into the warehouse, if—"

"Mercy, stop."

He felt her shake her head, sharply, negating any effort he might make at soothing her now.

"Don't you see? It's my fault he's dead. I was his partner, I should have been there with him, I could have done something—"

"Like die with him?" Grant said brutally, trying to break the rush of guilt that was pouring out of her.

"I could have—"

"Aren't you supposed to call for backup in situations like that?"

"Yes, but—"

"Then you did what you were supposed to do. Sounds like your partner didn't." He supposed it wasn't kind to say that about a dead man, but right now, all he could think about was Mercy, tough, indomitable Mercy, shaking with remembered horror and guilt.

"He was a senior officer. I should have followed him, not waited around to—"

"If you had, you'd be dead." His voice was flat, blunt, uncompromising. "Men like that grant no quarter. They'd have no more qualms about executing two of you than they had about one."

Grant wished she could believe him. It seemed so clear to him, as clear as a crystalline Wyoming winter day. There was nothing she could have done, except add herself to the murderers' list of victims. He supposed part of it was survivor's guilt, and the fact that she'd been so close to the murdered man only worsened the effect. But that wasn't all of it; she honestly thought she should have pulled off a miracle, that somehow she should have done the impossible.

But she wouldn't believe, wouldn't accept. He could sense it. She was too close to the victim, to what had happened. Too close to see it clearly. She was looking through a haze of pain and grief and guilt, and coming up with answers that were wrong, but seemed the only ones possible to her tortured mind.

"Do you remember that year when I came to visit Mom and went up into northern Minnesota, camping?" he asked softly.

As if wary of his seeming change of subject, she

hesitated before nodding; he felt, rather than saw, the movement of her head.

"I went hiking, up into the back country. On the second day, I saw a pack of wolves take down a deer. It was a young buck who'd gotten separated from the herd. It wasn't pretty, but while they were closed in for the kill, the rest of the herd escaped. There was no other choice for them. They didn't even have to think about choice—for them, the survival instinct is programmed in and undeniable. Only people get the idea that there's a choice to be made in situations like that. Sometimes I'm not sure that's a good thing."

"What...are you saying?"

"I'm saying that that buck got himself into that by straying from the safety of the herd."

She stiffened. "You're saying it was Nick's fault he got murdered? You're wrong. He may have been obsessed with...this case, because the cop who was killed was a friend, but he was still the best cop I ever knew."

He knew she was nowhere near ready to accept that her beloved partner just might have been partly to blame for what had happened to him, so he hastened to go on.

"My point is that just because you're in the city doesn't mean there aren't wolf packs, and they're just as ruthless there as they are in the wilderness. Worse, in fact, because wolves kill only for what they need to survive themselves. And if you'd given them the chance, these predators would have killed you, too. Is that what Nick would have wanted?"

She sagged against him again, and her whispered "No" was barely audible.

"Mercy, I'm sorry. I know you loved him, but getting yourself killed wouldn't have saved him, and thrashing yourself with guilt now won't bring him back."

"I did love him. He was...just about my best friend."

It seemed an odd way to describe a lover, he thought, but he said only, "I know how hard it is to lose someone you care for so much. What a hole it leaves."

She took in a breath, and he could almost feel her gathering herself together. And when she spoke, the harsh undertone in her voice was nearly hidden.

"I know you do. Your mother told Kristina she was genuinely worried about you when your father died."

Grant drew back slightly. "Was she? I didn't know. We never...talked about him much."

"She did love him, you know."

"Just not enough." There was little bitterness in his tone; that was something he'd worked hard enough at to be faintly proud of now.

"Enough to stay here? Perhaps not. But she did love him."

He sighed. "I know she did. But I don't think she ever regretted her decision."

"No. She told me once the only thing she ever regretted was not being with you as you grew up. And that if she hadn't been certain you were strong enough and independent enough and stubborn enough to make it on your own, she never would have been able to grab her second chance for happiness."

He chuckled. "She's sure called me the latter often enough."

He heard her make a small sound, not quite an answering chuckle, but light enough that he thought the initial storm just might be over. Then she gave a sigh that sounded more worried than anything, and he knew it was.

"I just hope Nick's kids are as strong as you were."

"He...had kids?"

"Two. A boy and a girl. God, it's going to be so awful for them, without him."

"I'm sure you'll...help them."

"I'll do what I can. I am their godmother, after all. But I'm afraid Allison's got a rough road ahead."

Godmother? What in the world? "Allison?" Grant asked, because he couldn't figure out what else to say.

"Nick's wife."

"He was married?" he asked blankly.

She lifted her head. "To one of my closest friends," she said, obviously puzzled. "I introduced them, in fact."

"But I thought..."

"You thought what?"

"Kristina said you were very close to him."

"I was." Her voice quavered just slightly. "I told you, he was just about my best friend. But he was...more than that. He was ten years older than I, and had been a cop for fifteen years. He was my mentor, the guy who got me through the toughest times of being a cop, and a female cop at that. He never coddled me, but he made sure I knew what I needed to know to make it. I was maid of honor at their wedding, and I was there when both Matt and Lisa were born. They were...family."

The emotional, clearly heartfelt outburst made Grant feel a bit slimy for his assumptions.

"I thought you and he were...you know."

"No, I don't know. What did you think—" She broke off suddenly, as if the obvious answer had finally struck her. "You thought Nick and I were... lovers?"

"Well," he said awkwardly, "yes. From the way Kristina talked..."

His voice faded away, and he wondered if he'd ever before felt so awkward, so much as if he'd really put his size eleven boots in his mouth. Both of them.

"She told you we were close, so you took for granted it was a...romantic relationship?"

"I—"

"Don't tell me you're one of those men who think a man and a woman can't simply be friends?"

"I never said that," he answered hastily, before she could take off on that tangent. "I just meant, from the way my sister talked, I...assumed. I shouldn't have. I'm sorry."

He was more than just sorry; his thoughts were in a horrible tangle. He was repelled by the brutality of what had happened, concerned over her feelings of guilt, sorry about his misguided assumptions...and unexpectedly and unwelcomely relieved to find that she and Nick hadn't been romantically involved. And he didn't like that reaction of his at all. He'd been able to keep his response to her under control when he was able to think of her as a woman grieving over the death of a lover.

But now, now that he knew Nick had been simply a friend, married to another friend, and that she was even godmother to their children, he wasn't sure where that left him and his confused emotions.

And he wasn't sure he wanted to know.

Six

She'd never thanked him for listening, Mercy thought. Not really. Not in the way she should have for what he'd done. No matter if you weren't personally involved, hearing such an ugly story wasn't easy. And it certainly wasn't Grant's business to listen to her, to let her pour out her agony as she had last night.

And, she added silently, color rising to heat her cheeks as she walked through the snow on this quiet, peaceful Sunday morning, it certainly wasn't his job to hold her as he had, so gently, so comfortingly, so…so tenderly.

Her mind shied away from the acknowledgment of what he'd done, and how she'd felt, how she'd let him, how she'd even relished the feel of his arms around her. Shied away from admitting he'd eased her pain as no one else had been able to do, simply by being there and holding her. And his words, so like what others had said to her, but somehow so much more powerful, had unexpectedly comforted her.

She knew it would take more than mere words to truly ease the guilt she couldn't help feeling, but for the first time since it had happened, she felt as if it were possible. Felt that someday, she might truly believe there was nothing else she could have done. And she found herself almost able to smile at the thought of her being romantically involved with Nick, who had been more of a big brother to her than anything. She could understand where Grant had gotten the idea, but not the odd way he'd reacted when he found out it wasn't true. He'd seemed almost...upset, and she couldn't come up with an explanation for that.

She looked out over the ranch, which was still covered with snow, although much had melted on this searingly clear day after the storm. She looked up at the Rockies, towering over the horizon with their own coating of new snow. She took in the quiet peacefulness of it, and she began to believe that just maybe she might be able to absorb some of this peace. That somehow the wild beauty of this land, where even the harshness of the kind of life where the only law was truly the survival of the fittest seemed clean and pure, might cleanse her tortured mind and heal her battered soul.

But it wouldn't do to become too fond of this place. She was only here until they caught the murderers, and then she'd be on her way back to the city, to help put them away and resume her life.

She heard the sound of a car, and glanced out toward the gravel lane that led to the ranch from the paved county road. She saw a bright red four-wheel-drive wagon approaching, its driver negotiating the snowy road with apparently little trouble. A local, she guessed before the probable identity of the new arrival struck her; Chipper's mother, the industrious, efficient and clever Rita, the more-than-accomplished cook.

Stop it, she muttered to herself. *You're be-*

ing...rude, she finished, not wanting to put the other probable name to what she was feeling.

Determined to chivy herself out of this silliness, she started back toward the house, determined to compliment the woman on the delicious food they'd been eating all week, thanks to her efforts. Even frozen and reheated, the meals of lasagna, meat loaf and chicken had been better than anything she'd ever managed on her own.

Her resolve to be gracious faltered slightly when she got close enough to see the woman; she was a brunette, all right, but she'd underestimated her flashing-eyed beauty. Rita Jenkins was nothing less than a stunner.

She also had her hands more than full, with a milk crate crammed with food, topped with several grocery bags, one of which seemed about to topple. Mercy hurried to rescue it.

"Oh! Thanks, dear. It would be the one with the eggs."

"Of course," Mercy said. She lifted another bag, and the dark-haired woman breathed a sigh of relief. "If not eggs, the bag with the most glass."

The woman's laugh was bright, cheerful, and charming, Mercy thought with an inward sigh. And the gleam in those dark brown eyes wasn't just beautiful, it was utterly delightful, with its warm humor. She also wore a simple gold wedding band on her left hand.

"I'm Rita," she said. "You must be Mercy."

"Not a tough guess, around here," Mercy said, but she made sure to smile as they lugged the bags inside and into the kitchen.

The laugh came again. "Grant told me you were coming. He neglected to mention how much you were going to pretty up the place."

Mercy blinked. "I...er... Thank you." She stammered to a halt, taken aback by the unexpected compliment.

"But," Rita added, "my son took up the slack. I believe you've made a conquest there."

"I...didn't mean to," Mercy said carefully as she set down her bags, not sure what to say; she knew Chipper had a crush on her, but this was his mother, after all.

"It's all right, dear. I'd worry, except for the fact that he falls in love an average of once a month."

"Oh. Good."

Rita laughed again, that bright, silvery sound. She was indeed a charmer, as much as Kristina was, although in a very different, much more earthy and open way. And she was, in her way, as beautiful as Kristina, the perfect dark foil to Kristina's blond beauty.

Suddenly Mercy felt very small and plain and mousy.

"Where's Grant?" Rita asked.

"I... He's checking on a pregnant mare. She's acting strange, Walt says."

"Must be Lady. Walt would know. He's the best horse midwife in the state."

Mercy couldn't help smiling at the thought of the crusty, grizzled old hand being called a midwife.

"I'd better get started," Rita said. "I was supposed to be here yesterday, but Jim didn't want me to drive all the way out here in that storm."

"Jim is your...husband?"

"That he is, lucky devil." Her voice lowered conspiratorially as she lifted out a can of tomato sauce. "Of course, I'm really the lucky one, but I'll never tell him that."

There was no doubting the sincerity of her words and her feelings, and Mercy felt a sudden lessening of pressure that bothered her as much as it relieved her. To hide what she was afraid might be showing in her face, she turned and began to empty another grocery bag. It was full of flour, white and brown sugar, butter and, at the bottom, bright red and green candy sprinkles.

"Christmas cookies?" Mercy guessed.

"Yes. For some reason, Grant said he wanted some this year. If I have time, I'll get to them today," Rita said. "I know it's a bit early, but getting out here this time of year is never certain."

She'd completely forgotten that Christmas was only three and a half weeks away; just getting through the Thanksgiving holiday with her concerned family had been enough to eat away all her slight emotional reserves. It was one of the reasons she'd agreed to come here; she hadn't thought she could deal with any more of her parents' fussing. They'd been worried a great deal about her, and although she understood and loved them for it, she found it more than a little wearing to have to constantly reassure them that she would be all right. Especially when she wasn't at all convinced herself.

"I...could do that for you. The cookies, I mean."

Rita's swift unpacking of the foodstuffs—she'd just lifted a sizable ham out of the plastic crate—came to a halt. She looked at Mercy, her expression for the moment unreadable.

"I don't mean to poach on your territory," Mercy said quickly. "It's just that I can't cook worth a darn, but cookies I can do."

Rita's bright smile flashed again. "I guess Grant's on his own with this ham he wanted, then. Maybe between the two of you, you can follow the instructions I wrote out." She set the large foil-wrapped piece of meat on the counter, then glanced at Mercy again. "Chipper says you're a police officer."

"Yes."

"That's a hard job. Seems like it would be even harder for a woman. In many different ways."

Mercy didn't see any point in denying it. "It is."

"Sort of like ranching in that, then. Harder on women."

Mercy blinked. "I...never thought of it that way, but I suppose you're right."

Rita set out the tomato sauce, some mushrooms and an onion, then took a package of pasta out of the last bag; they would be having spaghetti tonight, it seemed.

"Takes a certain toughness to make it out here," she said. "Most city folk don't have it."

"So I've been told," Mercy said wryly.

"Ah. Grant been riding that horse again, has he?"

"You could say that."

"He does have...a certain fixation." Rita reached beneath the stove for a large pan. When she straightened up again, she gave Mercy another sideways look. "And he has his reasons."

"I'm sure he does."

"Odd, though. You'd think, feeling that way, he'd make time for some of the local girls who are panting after him."

"He...doesn't?"

"Chipper says he never goes out with the boys. While they're out partying, he's back here doing whatever he does."

"You mean doing what it takes to keep a place like this going," Mercy said, not realizing until the words were out that she sounded a bit defensive.

Rita smiled, looking rather pleased. "Yes. It's a difficult job. It's not for everyone." She looked at Mercy steadily. "But it would be my guess that anyone tough enough to do your job could adapt to just about anything, if they wanted to."

Mercy met her look. "If they wanted to," she agreed, wondering exactly what Grant's reasons were.

Rita smiled again; it was wide and warm. "The cookies," she said, "are all yours."

"How did you get all the way up here?"

Mercy had heard Joker's familiar nicker a few moments ago, so she hadn't been surprised when Grant rode into view on the big Appy.

"I walked," she said. She was glad she was where she was, nearly at eye level with Joker; looking up at the tall man on the tall horse would have given her a neckache before long.

"That's quite a hike."

She couldn't argue with that; this high, rocky shelf that overlooked the ranch was nearly a mile from the house, most of it uphill. Fortunately, most of Saturday's snow had melted, so while the ground had been damp, she hadn't had to deal with that kind of heavy going.

And once she got here, the outcropping of rock that hung over the shelf had sheltered her from the wind even as it hid her from view, provided a soft place to sit on the bed of leaves and pine needles that had accumulated, and made her feel as if she had a private window out on the snowy world.

"I suppose. But I like it up here. It's…peaceful. Serene. Everything looks so clean, so quiet."

"I know," Grant said softly. "I used to come up here a lot. When my dad was sick, I used to…hide out up here, when things got to be too much."

"I'm…sure it helped."

The quiet admission had made something knot up inside her. And made her remember the gentle tenderness this man had shown her last night. That betraying heat begin to rise in her cheeks at the memory, and she went on hastily, lightly. "Anyway, I'm sure the exercise is good for me."

"At this altitude, if you did it without passing out, that's saying something." Grant crossed his arms over the saddle horn and leaned on it. He was grinning at her. "Around here, nobody goes more than fifty yards afoot unless they have to."

"Well," Mercy pointed out, "I have to, since I don't ride."

Grant's grin faded, and his expression became thoughtful. "That's not necessarily a good thing, exercise or not, out here. If anything happened, like a fall, you'd be in big trouble."

"How would riding help that?"

"Ranch horses don't fall often. They're sure-footed—rimrockers, every one of them."

"But first you have to stay on them," Mercy pointed out grimly.

"True." That grin that had taken her breath away when she was a child flashed; the effect hadn't been diluted much over the years. "But even if you don't, they'll head for home, and then we'll know we have a tenderfoot to go rescue. And I'd have to call Rocky out," he went on, clearly teasing now as he mentioned Jake and Erica Fortune's daughter Rachel, who, Kristina had told her, had opened an air search-and-rescue operation in Clear Springs before marrying Luke Greywolf, a local doctor. "And then Luke would worry, and—"

Mercy grimaced, cutting him off. "Thank you so much. But since I don't ride, this is all a moot point."

He seemed to hesitate, but then he said, "Maybe we should do something about that."

"About what?"

"You not riding."

Mercy blinked, and barely managed to keep herself from uttering a brilliant "Huh?"

Grant chuckled, she supposed at her expression. "Don't look so shocked. You must have thought about it. I know you have. You even said so."

"I...did?"

He nodded. "She did, didn't she, Joker? Said it right to your face."

The horse snorted, and Mercy gaped as the black head bobbed in apparent assent.

"That horse," she muttered, "is not normal."

"Hey," Grant said, clearly teasing now, "he remembers quite clearly when you told him he could make even a city girl like you want to learn to ride. That's not the kind of thing a guy forgets, you know."

Mercy eyed Grant warily. "Apparently not."

He grinned at her again. "Riding school opens in the morning. Be there."

"Grant, really—"

"I'm not a patient teacher," he warned, "so don't be late."

"Grant, be serious. I know you don't have time for this—"

"What I don't have time for is worrying about where you are or if you might have gotten hurt. Or riding all over to find out. So you learn to ride, and I stop worrying. Fair trade."

"You don't have to worry about me," she said, trying not to admit that the idea uncharacteristically appealed to her.

"Sure I do," he said easily. "Kristina'd slaughter me if anything happened to you."

Kristina. Of course. Mercy smothered a sigh, wondering what was wrong with her. She scrambled down from her perch, surprised as she left the shelter of the little alcove, at how much colder it was out here; she hadn't realized just how sheltered the natural formation was.

"Or, worse," Grant added as she landed near the stallion's feet, "she'd come out here and haunt me for the winter, and by spring I'd be stark raving mad."

"I thought you adored her."

"I do. But not here. She's far too citified to be

happy here, and when Kristina's not happy..." He let his words trail away with a shrug.

"So am I, as you've been at great pains to point out," Mercy said, annoyed by the snap that had come into her voice, but seemingly unable to stop it. She'd been right—the tall man on the tall horse was already making her neck hurt.

"I don't know," Grant said, as if pondering some deep mystery. "I'm beginning to think you might be trainable."

"Gee, thanks."

"Eight o'clock tomorrow. I've got to move some stock in off the high range at dawn."

"Grant—"

"Nod your head up and down, Mercy. Or you can walk back to the ranch."

"I was going to walk back anyway," she pointed out, rather acerbically.

"Yeah, but now you can ride. If you agree to be on time for class, that is."

What could it hurt? Mercy thought to herself. If you went to a ranch, wasn't it natural to learn to ride a horse? And it did look...appealing. And the freedom it promised—to be able, for instance, to get to this quiet, peaceful spot in half the time—was even more appealing. But—

"All right," she said, before whatever reservation her mind was about to throw at her could stop her.

"Good." Grant kicked his left foot free of the stirrup. "He's only been ridden double a couple of times, but it worked. Climb up."

Mercy eyed the stirrup, which on the big Appy was

above her waist. Then she gave Grant a wry look. "You're joking, right?"

"Oops. Sorry." He bent over and held out his left hand. "Just get your toe in, and I'll give you a lift. Come on."

She hesitated, finally got her foot up and into the leather-covered stirrup, then reached up to him. His hand locked around her wrist, and instinctively hers did the same. She felt his heat, the strong tendons and muscles beneath his heavy shirt and gloves, and... something else, something she couldn't name. She looked up at his face. He was staring at their hands, as if he'd felt the same odd sensation.

"Grant?" she said; it came out as barely a whisper.

He seemed to suddenly snap out of it. "Up you go," he said.

He did more than lift, he made it practically effortless, and almost before she knew it she was atop the horse. Who was much, much taller than she'd realized.

"Maybe this isn't the best idea after all," she said, eyeing the too-distant ground nervously.

"You're not afraid, are you? Macho cop that you are?"

"Macho," she said dryly, "I save for the misguided males of the species."

Grant laughed. "Hold on."

"How?" she asked. "You've got the stirrups. And the saddle. All I've got is...is..." The only word she could think of was one she didn't want to use.

"Hindquarters," Grant said blandly. "So you have to hang on to me. Haven't you ever ridden double on a motorcycle?"

"Even then I at least had pegs for my feet," she muttered.

"We'll stay at a walk. Won't we, Joker?"

The horse snorted and moved slightly at the sound of his name, and it took every bit of self-control Mercy had not to yelp. No, she thought as they started off, this was not one of her better ideas.

"This," Grant said in disgust, "is hopeless."

"I'm sorry," Mercy said meekly.

"I don't believe it. I've been working with horses all my life, and I have never seen anything like it."

"I'm not *doing* anything," she protested.

"Apparently," Grant said sourly as Joker trumpeted again, loudly, clearly annoyed, "you don't have to."

The gelding Mercy was astride, a horse Grant had said was normally one of the calmest animals on the ranch, danced nervously at the stallion's angry bellow. Shamelessly Mercy grabbed for the saddle horn; her pride wasn't about to go before a fall. She knew darned well she wasn't far enough along in her lessons after only three days to take much more of this.

"Maybe I should try to calm him down again," she suggested, rather lamely.

"Sure. And it'll last until you get on again. I don't believe it. The damn horse is jealous."

Mercy sighed. If Grant wasn't so clearly irritated, this whole thing would be rather amusing. Joker's annoyance with her riding lessons had been obvious from the beginning, and had become gradually more vocal every day. As silly as it seemed, the big Appy clearly didn't like the idea of her associating with other horses.

In a strange sort of way it was...flattering, she supposed. At least she had one male's full admiration on this ranch. Besides Chipper, of course, who continued to blush mightily every time he spoke to her, and who drove her crazy by constantly asking if there was anything he could do for her. But she couldn't really count Chipper. He was much too young. Younger even than the eighteen-year-olds she knew in the city. Or more likely, she thought with a sigh, the eighteen-year-olds she knew in the city were just older, aged by the too-frequent ugliness of their surroundings. She hoped Chipper knew how lucky he was.

She knew she was dodging the crux of the matter, that the real reason she wasn't counting Chipper's infatuation was the man standing here glaring at Joker. In the past three days, the forced closeness of these lessons—even when disrupted by Joker's irritation—had been unsettling, to say the least.

"He's rattling everybody's nerves," Grant muttered. "Even Gambler's taken off for the high country to get away from him. He's making every horse on the place nervous, and my hands are getting almighty tired of riding twitchy horses."

"Maybe we'd better stop, then," Mercy said, although she didn't want to give up; she'd found what riding she was able to do amid Joker's interruptions unexpectedly enjoyable and exhilarating, even within the confines of the big corral Grant had chosen as a classroom. But she tried to keep the disappointment from showing.

"I'll be damned," Grant muttered, "if I'll be buffaloed by a horse."

Joker neighed again, loudly, and Mercy's gelding danced skittishly. Grant grabbed the bay's bridle and held him steady. Mercy took the hint and slid to the ground; that she had learned early on. Joker whinnied once more.

"If I were the type to give animals human emotions," she said dryly, "I'd say he sounded rather smug that time."

"Believe it," Grant said. "He's pleased as all getout with himself."

Mercy walked over to the fence. Joker trotted over and nudged her eagerly, obviously proud that he'd managed to lure her away from that interloper. She couldn't help laughing, and she patted the horse's nose. He lowered his head with a gusty snort, and she reached up and tugged at his ear, an indignity the horse allowed with every appearance of pleasure.

"You're ruining my chance to learn to ride here, you big lunk," she told the horse sternly. "Thanks to you, I'm going to be housebound. All this gorgeous scenery, and I'm stuck looking at it from here."

"You really think it's gorgeous?"

She looked back over her shoulder at Grant, who was leading the little bay gelding. The horse eyed Joker nervously, but now that she was no longer in the saddle, the stallion seemed content to ignore his lesser colleague.

"Of course it is," she said. "How could anybody not think so?"

"Some don't," Grant said with a half shrug.

"Their loss," she said succinctly. Grant didn't answer, but she thought she saw something flicker in his eyes, something oddly both pleased and wary.

"Well, since it's his fault," he said, gesturing at the big Appy, "maybe he should pay the price."

"What do you mean?"

"I think he needs a refresher course in manners." He gave Joker a warning look. "And school is still in session."

"Uh-oh." Mercy gave the horse a look of mock concern. "I think you're in trouble."

"We'll see if he's still feeling so sassy after a few hundred circles around this corral. Come on."

Mercy frowned. "Me?"

"This saddle won't fit him," Grant said, nodding at the gear the bay wore. "Forks are too narrow. But the seat on my saddle's too big for you. We'll have to put my mother's old saddle on him, and the stirrups'll need to be raised. She's taller than you."

"Most people are," Mercy answered automatically. Then, as his meaning registered, her eyes widened. "Me? You want me to ride him?"

"I don't see any other solution. You still want to learn to ride, don't you?"

"Yes, I do, but I... He..."

"I know I should probably have my head examined. Normally I'd never trust a stallion of any temperament with a novice rider. But Joker's...different. And he's obviously protective of you, to say the least."

"But, Grant, he's so valuable to you—"

"He's a horse. And I don't believe in coddling them, no matter what they're worth. Joker works like any other horse on the ranch. It keeps him in line, keeps him from going soft.''

''But what if he gets hurt—?''

Grant grinned suddenly. ''You're too little to hurt him much.''

''Thanks,'' she said, her concern vanishing in a flood of the old irritation that she'd never quite been able to conquer when people assumed because she was small she was in some way inadequate.

''It's yourself you should be worried about. He's a lot more likely to hurt you than the other way around. Maybe you're right, we shouldn't do this.''

''I'll be just fine, thank you,'' she said, her tone as frosty as the snow that lingered in the shade of the trees and the buildings.

''Good. Then we can get on with this?''

Mercy opened her mouth to say an abrupt yes, then closed it before the answer came out.

''You did that on purpose.''

''Absolutely,'' Grant admitted, so blithely she couldn't help laughing.

''All right, all right. I suppose I don't mind being manipulated, as long as it's in a direction I want to go anyway.''

Despite Grant's reservations, in the days that followed Mercy found Joker to be a perfect gentleman, and much easier to ride than the little bay had been. Even his trot seemed less bone-jarring, and if she even felt the slightest bit as if she were losing her balance, the horse seemed to sense it and slowed to a stop.

''You've got him charmed, all right,'' Grant said, shaking his head in wonder on the fourth day of her lessons aboard the big stallion. But Mercy noticed he never took his eyes off the horse. Which meant, she thought edgily, that he never took his eyes off her, either.

She'd quickly realized what that inner warning had been that she quashed when Grant made the offer to teach her. Some part of her had known how difficult this was going to be, this forced proximity. Too frequently Grant halted the lesson and came to stand beside her to elaborate on some point, or to show her the proper position. And that seemed, all too often, to require him to touch her, to place her arms and legs where he wanted them, to make her stretch her heels down until she thought her calf muscles were going to ache for days.

But no amount of aching or stiffness—and she'd certainly suffered enough of that as she used muscles she'd never known existed before—could counteract the crazy little chills that seized her when he came toward her, or the darting blasts of heat that shot through her at his touch. And the fact that more than once she'd caught Grant staring at his own hands on her, or jerking them back as if burned by the contact between them, did nothing to allay her uneasiness.

She told herself it was simply that she was the only female around, and Grant was a red-blooded male. Sometimes, she thought, wishing she hadn't worked quite so much around men and so didn't know quite so much about them, he was an obviously red-blooded male, with that blood pooling in a place he was at some pains to hide. She told herself repeatedly she would be a fool to assume that his apparent arousal had anything at all to do with her, had anything to do with anything, besides her being the only woman around. He certainly hadn't done or said anything to make her think otherwise. Or to make her think his response was anything other than unwelcome to him.

It didn't help much. Not when her own body betrayed her so thoroughly. True, her response to him was far less visible—there were, it seemed some advantages to being female that she hadn't thought of before—but no less powerful. Her pulse sped up the moment she saw him, and when he touched her, even to tug mercilessly on her heels, she had an annoying habit of forgetting to breathe.

And the longer the lessons went on, the harder her reaction was to ignore. And Grant himself didn't look particularly happy; anytime one of those odd moments struck, when she would see him realize he'd been touching her longer than necessary, or staring at her without speaking for too long a time, he would pull back abruptly, avoiding her gaze, and stalk off like Joker in a sulk.

She wished they could just drag it out into the open, confront the unexpected thing that seemed to be happening between them. But she didn't know how to begin. Didn't know if she wanted to. Didn't know if she had the nerve to.

Perhaps, she thought with a sigh, it wasn't only riding lessons she needed.

Seven

Of all the stupid ideas he'd ever had in his life, teaching Mercy to ride had to be right up there with thinking Constance Carter would marry him.

And that, Grant added sourly to himself, was an incident he would do well to remember. He'd thought he had learned the lesson the sophisticated Miss Carter had taught him quite thoroughly, but apparently it needed reinforcing.

"Good night, Grant."

Mercy's voice was soft, quiet, and vibrant with that husky undertone that did crazy things to his pulse rate and made him continually have to suppress a shiver.

"Good night," he muttered.

He didn't look up at her. He didn't have to look to know what he would see; he'd been sneaking glances at her all evening. He knew how she looked, curled up on the sofa, wearing a soft pale green sweater of some fuzzy yarn over a dark green turtleneck and jeans. The color of her clothes seemed to make her eyes even more brightly green, her hair more golden. She looked...wonderful.

They'd both been sitting in the den reading all evening, her one of his volumes on horse husbandry, him the new technothriller that was somehow not managing to hold his attention at all. Occasionally she had asked him a question, each time apologizing for interrupting him until he told her to just ask and dispense with the guilt.

But after he'd explained his own completely unscholarly theory about why Appaloosas had shorter tails than most other horses—from their adaptation to the brushy country they'd originally sprung from under the careful guidance of the Nez Percé people, where a long, flowing tail would have been a nuisance—she fell to silent reading, and he was again faced with the fact that the book that normally would have held him rapt wasn't doing its job at all.

He sensed her hesitating in the doorway, and thought he heard a small sigh before she turned and walked away. A moment later, he heard her on the stairs, and then, finally, he heard the door of her room close.

He let out a breath he hadn't been aware of holding. Then his mouth curved wryly; why he was feeling relieved, he didn't know. A closed door between them—two closed doors, counting his own—didn't do a single damned thing to keep him from thinking about her, sleeping in the room right down the hall.

He'd been startled, even amused when it happened, that first night after she arrived, and he found himself waking from a dream in the middle of the night, a dream of her in the simple four-poster bed, curled up under the bright blue quilt. He'd chuckled, and ruefully admitted that he might have carried abstinence to the limit when he started thinking about the bane of his teenage years in such a suggestive way. Not that she wouldn't inspire that kind of reaction in a man who hadn't know the pest she had once been.

When it happened again, he'd been less amused. And as the dreams continued, growing more detailed—and uncomfortably more erotic—he'd become downright irritated. Whether at himself or the woman who seemed to be the cause of it all, he wasn't sure.

And then he'd had this stone-stupid idea about teaching her to ride.

He slapped his book closed with an angry motion. He let his head loll back on the recliner's cushion, his mouth tightening even further.

Didn't you think about it? he chastised himself. *Riding lessons, for God's sake. They require proximity. Talking. Touching. For extended periods.* He shook his head in self-disgust. *You walked into it with your eyes open, McClure. But apparently your brain wasn't connected.*

The answer suddenly struck him. He'd turn the lessons over to Chipper. He'd gotten her well started in the past week, and someone else could take over now. It was the logical thing to do. The boy, although a hard worker, was the least experienced of the hands, and therefore the most expendable. And he'd jump at the chance to spend two or three hours a day with the object of his current infatuation. And Grant could go back to running the ranch, mercifully free of Meredith Cecelia Brady's unsettling company.

Why hadn't he thought of this before? It was perfect. Very pleased with himself, he went back to his book. Realizing he'd absorbed absolutely nothing of the entire last chapter, he paged back to where he'd been when she asked him about Appaloosa tails.

Appaloosa tails.

Joker.

He couldn't turn the lessons over to Chipper. Not when she was riding the stallion that was the ranch's greatest single asset. No way could he lay that kind of responsibility on the kid. Nor would he. True, Joker had been more than a perfect gentleman from the beginning; in fact, he'd been almost unnaturally cooperative, stepping daintily, carefully, and stopping at the first sign of trouble, as if aware of the uncertainty of his rider. Some horses, and most stallions, would take that uncertainty as an invitation to rid themselves of that rider, but Joker had acted as if his only goal in life were to keep Mercy in the saddle.

That effort on the part of the stallion, plus her excellent physical condition and her exquisite sense of balance, had enabled her to progress much faster than Grant had ever expected. And as she had progressed in her riding, so had the easy rapport between her and the big Appy, to a point that amazed him; they were rapidly developing that rarest of things—that perfect communication between horse and rider that made simply watching them a pleasure.

But there was still no way Grant could leave the inexperienced Chipper alone to deal with Joker, should anything go wrong. Even if, as he suspected it would, Joker's conduct continued to be impeccable, the boy himself could make things worse by his own nervousness; he'd more than once mentioned to Walt that he didn't think he'd ever want a horse that valuable, because he'd be constantly worried about something happening to it. The poor kid would probably panic at the thought of dealing with Joker and Mercy at the same time.

Grant slammed his book closed again, knowing it

was useless. He was backed into a corner, just like that ornery bobcat he'd stumbled across in the hay barn last spring. And he felt about as amiable about the situation.

It was a long time before he could bring himself to make the journey upstairs, a journey that had never seemed so long before he had to pass that closed guest room door, thinking about the woman on the other side.

Mercy sat in the big blue armchair, her feet tucked beneath her and the quilt from the bed tucked around her, staring out into the quiet night. Once, she thought she heard the high, sweet up-and-down call of a meadowlark from the direction of the stand of tall cottonwoods on the far side of the mare's barn, but she decided she must be imagining it; surely the little birds had long ago headed south for the winter.

She let out a huge, breathy sigh, then nearly laughed at herself.

"Feeling mighty melancholy this morning, aren't you?" she asked rhetorically. Then she smiled, a soft, sad smile; that had been Nick's quiet way of nudging her out of whatever was bothering her.

Her breath caught. She sat motionless, waiting. The ripping, tearing pain didn't come. She still ached at the thought of her dead friend, tears still stung her eyes at the thought of his widow and children, she was still determined to do whatever was necessary to bring down his killers. But the ache didn't cripple her now, the tears didn't blind her...and, to her relief, the determination wasn't lessened by the easing of that vicious agony.

For a moment, she felt guilty, as if by allowing herself even this much healing she were betraying Nick's memory. But she knew it was a natural process, and knew as well that Nick wouldn't have wanted her to continue to grieve so fiercely for him. He would have been the first to tell her to get on with it, not to let his death stop her life.

Is that what Nick would have wanted?

Grant's words came back to her, and she knew now more than ever that he'd been right. Nick would no more have wished her to die along with him than he would have wished it on one of his kids. Or Allison. Not only because he'd come to like and care about her as much as she had him, but because there was another element in their relationship, unique to the job they did.

He'd as much as told her so, she remembered now, back on their first day on patrol together.

"If anything ever happens to me, you just keep your butt alive and get them. Put them away."

She had nodded, and managed a tight-voiced "You, too."

That had been five years ago. She'd never expected it to happen. Now it had. And she was here, instead of hunting down Nick's killers. The fact that she'd been ordered away didn't help much.

She sighed again, but much more quietly this time, as she looked out over the quiet landscape. The snow was nearly gone, but Grant had told her more was on the way, maybe even by tonight. She hadn't doubted him when he said he could smell it; he'd lived here all his life, and she figured he would know.

She would have thought that nothing could ease

such pain, that nothing could ever distract her from the devastating loss of her dear friend. But this place had. This place, and Grant McClure.

She could no longer, she admitted ruefully to herself, write this off as the lingering remains of her youthful crush. The boy she knew and adored twelve years ago had been bright, kind, and handsome. Not that Grant wasn't still all of those things, more so even, but now he had a man's strength, a man's determination, a man's quiet power.

And, she suspected, a man's scars.

The boy she worshiped had borne the scars of his divided family, but he'd told her himself he knew he was luckier than many; both his parents were reasonable, loving people, and he'd never doubted their love for him, even when their own failed.

But the man, she guessed, had been through his own, private wars.

He has his reasons, Rita Jenkins had said of Grant's fixation about city people. Mercy couldn't help wondering what those reasons were. And why the attractive woman seemed to already know. Had Grant perhaps figuratively—or even literally—cried on her shoulder?

She smiled slightly at the thought, realizing there was no longer any sign of the jealousy that had so unexpectedly struck her; it was impossible to be jealous of the straightforward, sincere woman.

Besides, her mind was suddenly full of the memory of how she herself had used Grant's offered shoulder to pull herself together in the wake of the horrid nightmare that had struck again, just when she thought she had beaten it back. Before, it had taken her hours to shake off the bloody images of Nick dying in her arms, the nightmare exaggerations of herself drowning in his blood, of Nick looking at her accusingly in a way he never, ever had in reality. But somehow Grant had managed to comfort her in a way no one ever had; somehow he had beaten the hideousness back for her.

He would have done it for anyone in her position, she told herself. Or for any friend of Kristina's. That she was both probably only meant that he would go well beyond the obligations of a reluctant host in his efforts to console her. It meant nothing more than that. It was a measure of his own kindness, and his love for his sister. It wasn't personal.

So why did he pull back as if he'd touched fire every time they came into contact? Why had she felt his gaze on her countless times last night as they sat in the den reading? She'd finally resorted to asking any idle question she could think of, just to stop herself wondering about it. Finally, it had been too much, and she'd fled to her room.

She'd still been lying awake when he at last came upstairs. She'd heard his careful tread on the steps, then down the hall, and told herself she was only imagining that he seemed to pause outside her door. And when she heard the door to the master bedroom close moments later, she hadn't known if she was relieved or disappointed. And that fact alone made her more edgy than anything else.

She blinked, suddenly becoming aware of what had been happening for a few moments now. Grant had been right on target. It was snowing. Quietly, steadily, the thick, fluffy flakes were falling straight down, with no sign of the wind that had blown them around in the earlier storm.

She watched for a long time, her inner peace seeming to grow as the snow again coated the world. Odd, she thought, that something could be so lovely, so serene, when you were safe and protected, able to look and see the beauty, and yet still be so dangerous if you were forced to try to survive out in it. Out there, it was hypothermia waiting to happen. From in here, where she was cozily warm, it looked like a Christmas card.

A Christmas card.

Again she'd forgotten how close the holiday was. And she'd done nothing, not even gifts for her parents, although they'd told her it wasn't necessary, under the circumstances. She knew they truly understood, but still she felt a twinge of guilt.

You're just feeling mopey, she chided herself. She knew that to a certain extent it was true; she'd always spent the holidays with her family, both Thanksgiving and Christmas, and missing the latter this year—for the reasons she was missing it—made her feel very isolated. But she knew it had to be; she didn't dare go to them. It seemed she'd accomplished her main goal by coming here, to this place where no one would ever think to find her, where no one could trace her, and she couldn't risk that by giving in to the longing to see her family again. She'd just seen them at Thanksgiving, she'd come up with a reasonable excuse for not coming back for Christmas, and there it had to stay.

But none of that made her feel any more comfortable about the fact that she was infringing here, that at a time of year that was meant to be shared with those closest to you, she was intruding on Grant's life. She'd known she would probably still be here, but somehow she hadn't thought about how it would make her feel.

And there wasn't a thing she could do about it. She couldn't go home, she couldn't go to her parents, she could only stay put. Dwelling on it would do no good. And moping around would only spoil everyone else's holiday cheer—or, worse, make them feel sorry for her.

Resolving to at least not ruin anybody else's celebration, she gathered up the quilt and scurried back to bed. She clenched her teeth against a shiver as her warm skin hit cold sheets, and curled up tightly until her body heat managed to warm things up. Thanks to the peace she'd found once more in the quiet, snowy splendor, she was asleep before it happened.

"How about that one?"

Mercy looked at the small but nicely shaped tree, then glanced back at Grant. "It's nice."

He knew she was picturing the little tree in the rather sizable living room.

"It's a little small," he admitted, "but I don't have much in the way of stuff to put on it. I think there are a couple of strings of lights somewhere in the storeroom, and maybe a box of ornaments my mother left behind."

Mercy's brows furrowed. "You think?"

"I haven't looked in a while."

"Walt said you don't usually have a tree. He seemed...surprised."

"Er...I didn't last year," he said, trying to divert her.

"Then why this year?"

"I just felt like it, okay?"

He knew he sounded a bit grumpy, but he didn't want to try to explain why he'd decided to put up a Christmas tree this year, when he wasn't sure he understood it himself. He dismounted and pulled the reins over his rangy buckskin's head to ground-tie him; the horse had been his primary mount before Joker's arrival, and he'd almost forgotten what a smooth stride the horse had. Not as smooth or as ground-eating as the Appy, but the buckskin was a good horse.

"Is it by chance the same reason you had Rita bring out that ham, when she said you don't even know how to cook one?"

"Just mind Joker, will you, while I cut the darn tree?"

He pulled the small ax he'd brought out of a saddlebag. They'd begun riding out only in the past three days, and while Joker's perfect manners had held, a lot more could go wrong out here than in the relative safety of the corral.

"Joker's fine. He and I have an understanding. What about the cookies?"

Grant looked back over his shoulder at her. "What?"

"The Christmas cookies. Rita said you asked for them especially this year."

"Rita," he said gruffly, "apparently had a lot to say."

Everybody seemed to have a lot to say about him,

he thought rather disgruntledly. Without further comment, he walked over to the small tree. He began to work on it with perhaps more industry than the fairly small trunk warranted. It kept him from having to reply to questions he had no answers for.

He didn't know why he'd felt this sudden urge to indulge in a few Christmas trappings. And he didn't like the way everybody seemed to read far too much into such a simple thing. Rita, Walt, even Chipper, they were all teasing him relentlessly. And now Mercy. Although she seemed more serious than teasing.

The buckskin gave him a wary look as he dragged the felled tree back, but settled down when he only took down his rope and tied it a safe six feet behind. It would drag easily enough and without much damage over the snow, he thought.

"Grant," she said, "if you—"

"Look," he said, cutting her off before she could start in on him again, "Christmas is just another day around here, the same work to be done, animals to be fed. So don't go reading anything into a silly tree and some cookies."

She just looked at him for a long, silent moment. Then, rather meekly—far too meekly for the Mercy he knew—she said, "I only wanted to ask if you'd mind if we went back by way of that place you showed me yesterday. By that little lake."

"Oh." He supposed he sounded as disconcerted as he felt.

"It's not too far from here, is it?"

"No. It's just over that rise." He had to give her

that much—for a city girl, she knew how to orient herself in new surroundings.

"So...can we?"

"Er...yeah. Sure."

"It won't hurt the tree?"

His gaze narrowed. Was she needling him? He couldn't tell. The woman, he'd discovered, was not only a lot more complex than the child had been, she was much more adept at hiding her thoughts. He'd been able to read the child fairly easily, but now he was never quite sure what the woman was thinking, unless her defenses were utterly down. Like that night in the barn.

And the kind of horror it had taken to bring her to that told him just how strong a woman the child had become.

"I'd just like to see it again. It was lovely."

Apparently she was having no such trouble reading him, Grant thought wryly.

"I'd think, being from Minnesota, you'd have seen hundreds of lakes prettier than that one."

"I can't explain," she said. "It just...seems special somehow."

"Then let's go," he said. He picked up the reins and swung back into his saddle.

The snow was deeper here in spots, and the going a bit heavier, but in just a few minutes they had topped the rise. The small lake was more like a large pond, nestled at the bottom of the rise. Beyond it, on the other side, was a flat that in summer was only sparsely dotted with sage, some patches of grass and the occasional spruce—not particularly interesting. But in winter, half iced over and surrounded by snow that turned even the rather monotonous sage into delicate crystal, and the spruce into majestic monoliths, and seen from the rise, it was the prototype for half the Christmas cards ever made.

Mercy swung her leg over Joker's back and dropped to the ground. She'd become quite adept at it, and with her fit agility she'd managed to work out a leaping method of mounting that bypassed the too-high stirrups. He'd teased her about becoming a trick rider, but she'd been too obviously proud of her progress—and rightfully so, he admitted—to take offense.

He dismounted himself, gauging as he stepped down that the snow was about six inches deep here atop the rise—not too bad. But more was expected soon, and he had the feeling that this time the white coat was here for the duration.

He stood slightly behind Mercy, watching. She said nothing, just stood looking out over the picturesque scene. The buckskin snorted and shook his head, while Joker lifted a forefoot and poked at the snow, pushing it into a little pile, either testing the depth himself or trying to build a snowman; Grant wasn't sure he'd put the latter past the clever Appy.

She stood there for a long time, not speaking, not moving, barely seeming to breathe, until Grant began to wonder if she was all right. At last he took a step forward, to where he could see her face.

She was crying.

It wasn't a noisy, wrought-up kind of crying. Her cheeks were wet, and tears were still flowing over them, but she was utterly silent. No sobbing, no wailing. It was as if the tears had simply welled up and overflowed. But that did little to allay his unease; he had little experience with weeping females, other than Kristina, who as a child had seemed to cry at the drop of a Stetson when she didn't get her own way. Fortunately, she'd outgrown that habit, as far as he knew.

But, as Mercy had pointed out, she was not Kristina. She never had been. It would take far more than a foiled childish want to make her cry.

"Mercy?" he said finally, unable to think of anything else to say.

She turned to look at him then. And to his surprise, what he saw in her eyes was not pain, or anguish, but a kind of glow that nearly took his breath away.

"It's so beautiful," she whispered.

"You're crying because...it's beautiful?"

Hastily she wiped at her cheeks, as if she'd become aware of her own tears only when he said it. "I'm sorry. Sometimes, when something...makes me feel so much, it kind of bubbles out."

"Don't apologize," Grant said, rather gruffly.

"I...I've learned to control it, most of the time. I have to, at work. But this...kind of snuck up on me."

Without even thinking of what he was doing—probably because if he had thought, he wouldn't have done it at all, he admitted—Grant put his arm around her. He felt her stiffen for an instant, and then she relaxed and leaned against him. She felt...good, there beside him. Right. Not too small, or too fragile, or too delicate for this tough land, but as if she fit, belonged.

And that she'd found so much beauty in this place that was his life made him feel...he wasn't sure what. Just as he wasn't sure what to call this odd sensation building inside him as they stood there in a companionable silence that was almost intimate. It wasn't just desire, although he'd at last had to ruefully admit that it wasn't simply long abstinence that had him wound up tighter than Walt's old pocket watch. It was so many other things, as well; respect for her courage, admiration for her intelligence and quick-wittedness, and appreciation for her willingness and ability to learn new things, even when they were utterly foreign to her.

It was a very confusing and unsettling mix, and he wasn't at all sure what it meant. In fact, he thought, he'd never been less sure about more things than he had been since Mercy walked back into his life.

Except for the unexpected fact that the child who had turned his summers into chaos seemed to have become a woman capable of doing the same to his entire life.

Eight

"You're what?"

Grant stared at Walt, who returned his gaze with a twinkle lighting his eyes that Grant didn't trust at all.

"You heard me," the old hand said.

"But you never go to town for Christmas."

"I told ya, they're having a big wingding over at the cattle growers' building. Dancin' and all. Saw the posters for it when I was in town last week. Probably go on all night."

"They do that every year," Grant pointed out, "and you've never gone before."

"Maybe I never been asked before," Walt said blithely.

"But—"

"You saying I can't have Christmas Eve off? Just because I don't have family around here like the rest of the men, does that mean I can't make plans? Downright Scroogey of you, boy."

"Of course you can," Grant began, "but—"

"I'll get my chores done 'fore I leave, and make sure all the animals are handled and bedded down. Even you should be able to handle the rest."

"It's not that—"

"And besides, you'll have Mercy here to help. Wouldn't say that, usually, but for a city girl she's picked up right fast on things.'' Walt grinned suddenly. ''A lot of things.''

''Yeah,'' Grant muttered.

''A diamond's a diamond, boy, no matter where you find it, or what kind of setting it's in, fancy or plain. And all the fancy trappings in the world don't make a diamond outa glass.''

Grant grimaced. ''You want to quit philosophizing and say what you mean?''

''I mean you're as stubborn as a mule and blind as a bat about city girls,'' Walt said, his tone stern. ''And if you ask me, I think you're afraid of bein' all alone out here with that little gal.''

''Don't be ridiculous,'' Grant snapped, wondering if it sounded as unconvincing as he felt.

''Ridiculous? I may be old, son, but I ain't blind. Anyone can see—''

''Whatever they want to see.''

This time it was Grant who cut the other man off, not wanting to hear what the old hand thought everyone could see. He already knew, anyway. He'd caught enough surreptitious glances and stifled grins from all the hands to have a pretty good idea of what they were thinking. And the fact that more than once one of them had caught him intently watching Mercy as she rode, or as she tended to Joker—she'd insisted that if she was going to ride him, she would take care of him, as well—or as she did another of the small chores that accumulated, to make his and everyone's life so much easier, didn't help any.

It was just that he was...intrigued, Grant insisted to himself as Walt walked away, chuckling. Mercy had adapted to life here better than he'd ever expected her to. Better than he would have expected any city girl to. Certainly better than Kristina ever had on even her fair-weather visits. But then, he hadn't expected Kristina to adapt. She was a—

Stubborn as a mule and blind as a bat about city girls...

Walt's words echoed in his head, but he told himself the man who'd known him longer than anyone except his mother was wrong. He wasn't blind, or stubborn, he was just...wary. And with good reason.

Annoyed—he told himself it was with Walt's meddling, but he had a suspicion that he was kidding himself—he strode out of the tack room and toward the house. He headed for the side door to the mudroom outside the kitchen. Once inside, he pulled his coat off first, then boots wet from a day slogging around in the snow, breaking up the ice that had formed on the three natural water holes on the flats; the last thing they needed was to have to rescue unwary cattle who had strayed too far out on the thin ice in search of water.

Even his socks were soaked, he thought wearily, and he supposed his feet had been colder than this sometime in his life, but he couldn't recall when right now.

He sat on the small bench in the mudroom, for a moment too tired even to stand and go into the warmth of the house. But soon the chill overtook even his weariness, and he knew he needed to move. In a minute, he'd be shivering.

He stood up. His icy feet protested, and he knew he should get inside. But he'd become aware of something else now, more baking smells drifting from the kitchen. Mercy hadn't been kidding; she might not cook, but she could bake up a storm. Everybody on the ranch had been spoiled by her delicious bread, biscuits and cakes. He wondered if she worked this hard when she wasn't trying to keep her mind occupied; he had a feeling she did. She did it too naturally; whether it was one of the inside chores he had a tendency to let slide, or outdoors, doing hard, dirty work, she brought to it the same energy and determination.

He opened the inner door and stepped into the kitchen. Cookies, he thought, recognizing the smell in the instant before he saw the obvious proof in the gaily decorated shapes cooling on the counter. Christmas cookies.

Mercy, traces of flour on her clothes and smeared across one cheek, gave him a smile that warmed him as much as the change in temperature between the two rooms. She gestured with the baking sheet dotted with cookie dough that she held in one hand, indicating the already sizable piles of still-warm freshly baked treats.

"Rita said you asked about having cookies this year. I hope you meant it."

"I..."

His voice trailed off; he couldn't think of a thing to say. He'd only mentioned it because he vaguely remembered his mother making cookies, probably when he'd been barely big enough to toddle around in this same kitchen, and he'd thought it might take away some of the glumness of spending the holiday away from home and her family.

Mercy slid the baking sheet into the oven, shut the door, then tugged off the oven mitt she'd been wearing. Grant heard a sound from the corner of the room, and glanced over to see, to his shock, Gambler sitting there, waiting patiently. What he was waiting for became obvious when Mercy tossed him a piece of a broken cookie. The dog caught it neatly, gulped it down, and settled in to wait for the next.

"Even the dog," he muttered.

"What?"

"Nothing."

Why was he surprised? After Joker fell for her like a ton of horse, why shouldn't Gambler do the same? Even the little Aussie dog's cool aloofness was no match for Mercy's genuine warmth and the sincerity that radiated from her.

"You look cold," she said.

"I am," he admitted.

"Chipper told me you'd probably come in cold and wet."

Grant's brows lowered. "He's supposed to be riding fence today."

"He is. He just came by to tell me his mother wasn't going to be able to get here because his little sister was sick, so I should go ahead with the cookies without her." She grinned. "He looked a little eager for them himself."

"I can see why," Grant said; he'd never seen so many cookies at once before. But he knew that once the hands found out about them, they'd disappear rapidly. If there were any left at all for Christmas Eve tomorrow, he'd be surprised.

Not, he thought, that there'd be any need for them. Not with just him and Mercy left on the ranch, while everybody else scattered for their own personal celebrations.

I think you're afraid of bein' all alone out here with that little gal.

An odd contraction of muscles rippled through him; Grant told himself he was shrugging off Walt's silly assessment, but it might have been a shiver, as well. Strictly because he was cold, he insisted silently, even though the kitchen was cozily warm.

"You *are* cold," Mercy said. "Here, munch on these and wait a second."

Before he could speak, she'd shoved three fragrantly warm cookies at him and disappeared into the utility room on the other side of the big kitchen. It contained the big chest freezer, the laundry facilities and a washtub and counter, among other things, and had an outside door so that the hands could get in and use the heavy-duty washer and dryer if they wanted to. As he took a careful bite out of one of the rich butter cookies—and then gobbled down the rest—he heard what sounded oddly like the clothes-dryer door opening, then closing, and only then realized that he'd been hearing the appliance's faint hum since he'd walked into the kitchen.

He was considering whether to snag one of the rather intriguing-looking snowman cookies when Mercy came back, holding something in her hands.

"Here," she said, holding out to him what looked like a pair of his own heavy wool socks.

"What—" He broke off abruptly the moment he touched them; they were warm, almost hot. Fresh from the dryer, he realized.

"Put them on. Now, before they lose all the heat."

SILHOUETTE®

AN IMPORTANT MESSAGE FROM THE EDITORS OF SILHOUETTE®

Dear Reader,

Because you've chosen to read one of our fine romance novels, we'd like to say "thank you"! And, as a **special** way to thank you, we've selected <u>four more</u> of the <u>books</u> you love so well, **and** a very nice Surprise Gift to send you absolutely _FREE!_

Please enjoy them with our compliments...

Senior Editor,
Silhouette Intimate Moments

P.S. And because we value our customers, we've attached something extra inside ...

PEEL OFF SEAL AND PLACE INSIDE

HOW TO VALIDATE YOUR
EDITOR'S FREE GIFT "THANK YOU"

1. Peel off gift seal from front cover. Place it in space provided at right. This automatically entitles you to receive four free books and a free Surprise Gift.

2. Send back this card and you'll get brand-new Silhouette Intimate Moments® novels. These books have a cover price of $3.99 each, but they are yours to keep absolutely free.

3. There's no catch. You're under no obligation to buy anything. We charge nothing — ZERO — for your first shipment. And you don't have to make any minimum number of purchases — not even one!

4. The fact is thousands of readers enjoy receiving books by mail from the Silhouette Reader Service™ months before they're available in stores. They like the convenience of home delivery and they love our discount prices!

5. We hope that after receiving your free books you'll want to remain a subscriber. But the choice is yours — to continue or cancel, anytime at all! So why not take us up on our invitation, with no risk of any kind. You'll be glad you did!

6. Don't forget to detach your FREE BOOKMARK. And remember...just for validating your Editor's Free Gift Offer, we'll send you FIVE MORE gifts, *ABSOLUTELY FREE!*

THIS SURPRISE MYSTERY GIFT CAN BE YOURS _FREE_ AS ADDED THANKS FOR GIVING OUR READER SERVICE A TRY!

THE EDITOR'S "THANK YOU" FREE GIFTS INCLUDE:

▶ Four BRAND-NEW romance novels
▶ PLUS — a very nice added gift

YES! I have placed my Editor's "thank you" seal in the space provided above. Please send me 4 free books and a free Surprise Gift. I understand I am under no obligation to purchase any books, as explained on the back and on the opposite page.

245 CIS A7UR (U-SIL-FC-04/97)

NAME

ADDRESS   APT.

CITY   STATE   ZIP

Thank you!

THE SILHOUETTE READER SERVICE™: HERE'S HOW IT WORKS

Accepting free books places you under no obligation to buy anything. You may keep the books and gift and return the shipping statement marked "cancel". If you do not cancel, about a month later we will send you 6 additional novels, and bill you just $3.34 each plus 25¢ delivery per book and applicable sales tax, if any*. That's the complete price, and—compared to cover prices of $3.99 each—quite a bargain! You may cancel at any time, but if you choose to continue, every month we'll send you 6 more books, which you may either purchase at the discount price…or return to us and cancel your subscription.

*Terms and prices subject to change without notice. Sales tax applicable in N.Y.

He obeyed without another word, sighing aloud at the warmth. When he looked back at Mercy, she was smiling widely.

"My mom always used to do that when I came in with frozen toes from playing in the snow. It always felt so good."

"It still does," Grant said fervently.

"Of course, now she just makes me sit down and pour desert sand out of my shoes when I come in."

"Quite a change from Minneapolis snow."

"Yes. But they like Arizona. And it is beautiful there. When the brush is green, and the Dragoon Mountains are looking really red, it's lovely. Besides, my dad gets a kick out of telling people they live just outside of Tombstone, and can see Boot Hill from their backyard."

He smiled at her words, but wondered if there was an undertone of sadness in them. Or loneliness.

"You must...miss being with them now."

She leaned against the edge of the large cooking island. His father had had the old, smaller kitchen remodeled for his mother as a wedding present; later, after she left, he'd barely been able to bear sitting in the spacious, efficient room. It hadn't been Grant's favorite place, either, but now, full of the aroma of baking and with Mercy standing barely two feet from him, it seemed the coziest room in the house.

Mercy tossed another bit to the waiting Gambler. He snapped it up, then looked at her questioningly.

"That's it, sweetie," she said. "Any more might make you sick."

The normally reserved dog wagged his stump of a tail, but seemed to understand. He glanced at Grant, as if gauging his owner's mood. Grant wasn't sure what the dog saw, but apparently it wasn't enough to drive him away; he curled up on the rag rug in front of the sink and closed his eyes. If the dog didn't work so darned hard, he'd think he was getting soft. But he deserved a little spoiling, Grant thought, if he'd take it. And apparently Mercy's charm extended to the dog, as well as the horse.

Then, finally, after he decided she wasn't going to, she responded to his statement about her parents. "I do miss them. But I was just there at Thanksgiving. And I knew I couldn't...take much more of their well-meaning concern."

"Kristina said you needed someplace where people wouldn't...talk about it all the time."

"And you've given me that." She looked up at him earnestly. "Thank you for that, Grant."

"I... You're welcome. But I should be thanking you, for all you're doing around here. I told you didn't have to work—"

"And I told you I needed to."

"I understand."

She looked at him for a long moment. "Yes, I think you do. And I thank you for that, too. And for all the quiet, peaceful places you've shown me here. I know it took up a lot of your time, taking me all over—"

"They're places I love. It's no hardship."

And it hadn't been. He'd found a new appreciation of things he sometimes took for granted, seeing them anew through her eyes, experiencing the peace they could bring all over again, simply by watching the calm spread over her face and the shadows retreat from her eyes.

"I thank you, just the same."

"I should thank you. I needed them, too, once. You made me see them again. Regain what they mean to me."

"Grant," she said, whispering his name, as though her throat had become suddenly tight.

"Mercy," he said. His voice sounded the same.

He wasn't sure how it happened. He didn't remember moving, but he didn't remember seeing her move, either. But then she was in his arms, his hands had tilted her head back and he was lowering his head, his mouth searching for hers hungrily. He heard her make a sound, not of protest, but of surprise. And then she was helping him, stretching up to meet him, to span the distance between them.

Her lips were soft, warm, and a haven after the chill of the day. She tasted of sugar and cookies, and something else hot and sweet and distinctively Mercy. Somehow he'd known she'd taste like this.

What he hadn't known was how just the feel of her mouth under his would send a heat rocketing through him that vanquished any lingering chill he'd brought inside with him. What he hadn't known was how the feel of her petite body pressed against his like this would make him resent the layers of clothing between them. What he hadn't known was how kissing her would send him into a whirling spin, knowing nothing but the feel and taste of her and not caring.

What he hadn't known was that kissing her wouldn't ease the ache that had been building in him for days, but instead would expand it, so fiercely and so suddenly that he doubted he could contain it much longer.

He had to stop this. He had to, he knew he had to; much more of this, and he was going to die if he didn't have her, right here, right now. She had him so fired up, he didn't think he could even make it to the floor; it would be right here on the damned kitchen counter. Not that that wouldn't work nicely, with his height and her lack of it...

With a throttled groan, he made himself pull back. Had he thought this room cozily warm? It seemed downright cold now, without the heat of her, without the touch of her mouth, without the feel of her curves pressed against him.

He heard her make a tiny sound, half sigh, half... He didn't know what. He only knew he felt like whimpering himself.

Mercy groped blindly for the edge of the counter. She looked up at him. Her eyes were wide and stunned-looking. He knew he should say something, do something, but he couldn't seem to manage either.

Mercy swallowed, the movement visible at her slender throat.

"I..."

She swallowed again and tried again. This time she was more recovered, and her words came almost normally, with just an undertone of wobbliness.

"When you say thank-you, you don't kid around."

Grant blinked. He supposed quick recoveries were a necessary part of her work, but he wasn't sure he liked this one.

"That," he growled, "had nothing to do with thank-yous."

"Grant—"

"Thank-yous are for...cookies." He turned on his heel, and added, "And warm socks."

He walked away without looking back, telling himself he was in a hurry to get into more warm, dry clothes than just his socks. But he didn't believe it, not when he knew perfectly well that he was fleeing from the kitchen like a kicked puppy, because if he stayed he was going to kiss her again, and he didn't want to have to answer for what might happen if he did.

She wondered if he was going to come in at all. She knew, because he'd told her often enough, that the ranch neither knew nor cared that it was a holiday eve; the same work had to be done as on any other day. And it would be the same again tomorrow, Christmas Day.

But she also knew that Walt had done most of the chores before he hopped in the truck this morning and drove off toward town, Chipper beside him, headed home for a celebration only slightly marred by his little sister's bout with the flu. The rest of the hands had—most of them stopping by to get a handful of cookies to tide them over on their journeys, and to leave her with some rather surprising tokens—been gone by noon, some riding, most piling in large groups into the two other available ranch vehicles, each driven by the man who had the farthest to go, who would reverse the trip the morning after Christmas Day, picking up the hands he'd dropped off today.

But Grant was still holed up in the tack room. He'd told her there would be no lesson today, rather gruffly, and apart from that he'd barely spoken to her.

He certainly hadn't mentioned what happened in the kitchen yesterday. And she couldn't decide if she was hurt or relieved. How could she, when she was still in shock? Never had she felt anything like what she'd felt when Grant kissed her. None of the imaginings she'd ever had, rising out of childish ignorance of what happened between a man and a woman, had ever been anything like this. Even what she'd experienced as an adult, although admittedly limited, had never, ever led her to believe that a single kiss could have the effect this one had had.

And there had been nothing of the infatuated child in that kiss. It had been purely adult woman, responding to adult male. The woman who had been trying so very hard to wish away the effect this man had on her. The woman who finally had to admit that the boy she'd had the huge crush on had become the man who could shake her to the core with a single kiss.

She took in a deep breath and held it for a moment. She didn't know what to do now, but couldn't help feeling that she should do something. Anything. And feeling that if she didn't, she would soon be flying out of her skin. She was already pacing the floor of the living room, and she found herself checking the wood stove every five minutes despite the fact that she'd just added two sizable logs to it.

She made herself sit down on the comfortable old couch, just to stop herself from that fruitless crossing and recrossing of the room. She took in another deep breath, trying to steady herself. But it did little good, not when the air was scented with the fresh fragrance of the tree they'd brought home, now sitting in front of her, barely a yard away.

She remembered that long, quiet time at the small lake, when Grant had put his arm around her in quiet understanding. She'd known then that he, too, had sought out the quiet places to heal his pain. And that he knew she needed the same kind of peace those places had given him. On the heels of that thought came the memory of the way he'd thanked her.

I needed them, too, once. You made me see them again. Regain what they mean to me.

It took a strong, secure man to admit that he needed something as ethereal as the peace of quiet, lonely places. But then, she'd had no doubts that Grant was a strong man. She'd known—sensed, somehow— even when he was sixteen that he had within him that kind of strength. It was the other part that had her mind racing. Was it simply because he was secure enough not to care what anyone else thought? Or had he admitted to that need because he knew—and trusted—that she would understand?

Do you have to analyze everything, Brady?

Nick's wry voice came back to her, and she felt a sudden return of the old pain as she thought of his family, spending their first Christmas without him. That was where she should be, she thought. She should be with them, with Allison and the kids, her godchildren. But she knew it was impossible, and the Corellis knew why it was. They probably understood better than anyone. Allison had been among the first to encourage Mercy to come here, to put a safe distance between herself and the city. But that didn't remove the feeling. And she wasn't sure she was any better off thinking about that than she had been trying to figure out Grant's motives.

Maybe she did analyze too much, but if it was a weakness, it was also one of her strengths; more than once, it had provided a lead that had paid off. Even Nick had to admit that, although it had been more frequent that he just gave her a sideways look and said, "Sometimes, Brady, a cigar is just a cigar."

And sometimes, Mercy thought as she glanced out the window, where the afternoon shadows had turned to dusk, men were a pain in the backside.

Even as she thought it, her own particular pain in the backside opened the front door and stepped inside, Gambler at his heels. The boss and the dog got no days off, it seemed, though everyone else had abandoned them for their own revelries.

She watched as he took off his hat and coat and hung them on the rack just inside the door; he was drier today than yesterday, it appeared. Then he turned back and leaned down to pick something up off the porch. When he came inside, she saw that it was an armful of pine branches.

He stopped when he saw her sitting there, as if he hadn't realized she was there. For a moment he just stood there, as if he weren't sure what to say. Then, at last, he gestured with the branches.

"I thought we could use the fireplace tonight, and add them to the fire. This stuff smells good when it burns."

Yet another addition to the list of little things he'd done, she thought, including saving and setting out as decoration the Christmas cards he'd received from his family and neighboring ranchers, when Walt had told her they were usually read and discarded as soon as Grant was sure he'd returned the favor. That, the tree, the cookies...were they all for her sake, these concessions to the holiday that the other ranch residents' reactions told her were so uncharacteristic?

He stacked some logs in the grate of the fireplace, then tossed a couple of the pine branches and some kindling on top and underneath and lit the whole pile. It caught quickly, and in minutes the distinctive scent began to waft into the room. He turned back, and simply stood there for a moment. Yesterday—before he'd kissed her, anyway—she would have suggested he sit down and relax. Now she didn't quite know what to say.

At last he walked toward her and sat on the couch beside her. Well, sort of beside her, Mercy amended in rueful silence; he'd left a safe three feet between them. Gambler curled up on the hearth rug before the fire and promptly went to sleep, unaware of or choosing to ignore the undercurrents between the humans in the room.

She'd heated up Rita's contribution to the evening, a heaping plate of spicy chicken wings and a huge pot of homemade soup. Grant tackled it hungrily. And silently.

"Would you like something warm to drink?" she asked when he paused for a breath.

He considered this for much longer than she thought the simple question deserved, then finally nodded. She got up and went to the kitchen, where she'd had her usual Christmas Eve concoction heating. After a few moments of preparation, she had the two glass mugs ready and walked back into the living room. Grant took his and sniffed curiously.

"Hot apple cider?"

"Sort of," she said. "It's a tradition in my family."

Looking curious, he stirred the golden liquid with the cinnamon stick she'd put in it, then put the mug to his lips. He took a sip. His brows shot up, but then he licked his lips, as if he liked the taste.

"Brandy?" he asked.

"What? Oh, yes. Brandy." She hoped the flush she felt in her cheeks would be written off to the warmth of the brew, or at least the crackling fire, rather than it's true cause, watching Grant's tongue slide over his own lips as it had over hers yesterday. "I hope you don't mind."

"No, I'm just surprised. I didn't know we had any."

"Walt got the things for me when he was in town last week."

"Oh." He took another sip, longer this time. Then he smiled. "This is really good."

"I'm glad you like it."

He sipped again, this time looking at the tree. "Where did all that come from?" he asked, indicating the odd assortment of things hanging on the tree, from a polished silver spur to a small golden cross.

"The hands," she said simply. "They came in to trade them for cookies, to dress up the tree."

His startled gaze flicked to her, then back to the tree. "Oh" was all he said. "It looks nice."

She supposed they could be having a more mundane conversation, but she wasn't positive. But a few moments later, as silence returned between them, she thought she would have welcomed even prosaic conversation. Or perhaps it was only her imagination that told her the silence was a strained one; that faculty had certainly been working overtime lately. She'd even thought perhaps he had another reason for lighting the fire in the seldom-used fireplace, that it might have something to do with the fact that an open fire was a lot more...enjoyable than a closed wood stove. And she refused to acknowledge the word she hadn't used, even in her thoughts.

Grant finished his meal, and Mercy gave up on hers; she'd managed to down only a small bit of the tasty soup and a couple of the spicy chicken pieces. He cleaned his hands and then tossed the napkin into the fire. They both watched the blaze as the paper caught and burned as if it were a major solar flare-up and their job was to study it.

Mercy wasn't comfortable with the silence that spun out once more, but she couldn't think of a thing to say that wouldn't probably make it worse.

"Do you want to go for a ride tomorrow?"

Mercy blinked, almost as startled by the suddenness and sound—as if he'd been trying to speak—of his words as by what he'd said.

"I thought you said—"

"I know. But Joker's already antsy after one day off. If he gets another, he'll be crazy."

"Oh." Of course. Joker. That was the reason for the request, not any desire to ride with her, or even to see that she got out on Christmas Day. "We can't have that, can we?"

She hadn't thought she sounded particularly sarcastic, but still he looked at her rather sharply. And spoke the same way.

"If you don't want to, I'll take him out."

She sighed. "I didn't mean that. I'd like to go for a ride. It sounds like a lovely way to spend Christmas morning."

"All right, then."

"But not," Mercy went on, "if you're going to act like a cranky grizzly bear all day."

"Grizzlies are always cranky," he said, a snap still in his voice. "It's their nature."

"So sue me for a redundancy."

His mouth tightened, but he didn't speak. He finished his drink. He tugged off his boots. He got up and threw another log on the fire, which didn't need it yet. All without saying another word. She half expected him to leave while he was up, but he came back and sat down again. She let out a small breath of relief.

Hard to believe, she muttered to herself, *that you once got a medal for valor.*

Her own chiding sarcasm roused her to speak.

"Is this about yesterday?"

Grant froze. Then, slowly, he turned his head to look at her. "What?"

"Your...mood. Is it about what happened in the kitchen yesterday?"

She saw his jaw tighten. "You mean kissing you?"

It took nearly all her nerve to nod.

"No."

She breathed again, once more not sure if she was relieved or disappointed. *Delusions of grandeur, Brady,* she muttered to herself. *Whatever made you think that, just because that kiss boiled your blood, it did a thing for him?*

"It's not about kissing you at all," Grant said.

Did he have to rub it in, that she'd been a fool to even think it might have been? "Fine. I'm sorry I even thought it might be—"

"It's about," Grant said, sounding rather ominous, "the fact that I didn't want to stop with a kiss."

Nine

Grant regretted the words the moment they escaped, but it was too late. He couldn't call them back.

To hell with it, he swore inwardly. He was tired of trying to hide the fact that he wanted her. He didn't even know why he'd been trying. He'd taken worse teasing from the hands before, and no doubt would again.

And it was only natural, he told himself. Even likely. You take a healthy thirty-year-old guy, stick him out on a remote ranch with nothing but cattle, horses, a scruffy dog and some ranch hands for company, then drop a gorgeous woman like Mercy in the middle of it—what do you expect? There was every reason to count on exactly what had happened. And no reason to try and hide it.

Except that the woman who'd been dropped in the middle was here to heal, to grieve over the ugly death of a dear friend. Hardly in a state to be rational. Or make a rational choice. To take advantage of that would be contemptible.

Not to mention dangerous, he thought wryly, if Kristina ever found out. Fortunes, he'd learned, were a very tempestuous breed. Perhaps, he thought, suddenly serious as he remembered Nate's brother, Jake, even murderous.

But Mercy wasn't. She was merely...vulnerable. And right now she was blushing furiously.

"I'm sorry," he said, a little stiffly. "I didn't mean to embarrass you."

"I... You..."

"Forget I said it, will you?"

She bit her lip. Then her chin came up, as it always seemed to when she was confronting something difficult head-on. Which was most of the time; no side-stepping or tiptoeing around for Mercy, even if the subject was unpleasant.

"Only if you didn't mean it."

He drew back slightly. "What?"

"Is it true?"

"Mercy—"

"Very simple, a yes-or-no question. Is it true?"

"You were there," he said dryly. "What do you think?"

"I don't know. I don't have...a lot of experience in this. At least, not recently."

"Oh, God," Grant muttered.

"Did you...not want to stop?"

"Damn it, Mercy—"

"Did you?"

"I was as hot as that damn oven," he snapped. "Does that answer your question?"

Her color deepened. "I...suppose so."

She turned her eyes back to the fire. She stared into the flames. He wondered what had possessed him to kindle the blaze in the first place. Either blaze, the one on the hearth or the one between them.

She said nothing. She simply sat, watching the shifting golden light, not even jumping as an occasional pocket of resin in the pinewood he'd added heated up and snapped like a gunshot. But then, he supposed that sound was probably as distinctly unlike a shot to her as Gambler's howl was from a coyote's to him.

She still said nothing. What the hell was she thinking? How could she prod him into an admission like that and just...sit there?

"That's it?" The words finally burst from him, despite his efforts to match her apparent calm. "You ask a question like that and just leave it there?"

She turned her head. Her cheeks looked faintly pink, but no more than they might be from the heat of the fire just a couple of feet away.

"I just needed to know if..."

"If what?"

She lowered her eyes then, and he knew the blush was coming from the inside. "If I was the only one who was...feeling that way."

Grant sucked in a deep, harsh breath. "I... You... didn't want to stop, either?"

As if she'd just realized she was avoiding looking at him, her head came up again. And again Grant silently saluted her; she might be a city girl, but she wasn't short on pure nerve. No wonder she was good at her job, difficult though it was.

"As scary as it is...no. I didn't want to stop."

"Mercy," he began, but broke off when he heard the tight, urgent sound of his own voice. His body had reacted to her simple admission with a violent swiftness, and he needed all his concentration for a moment to rein in the heat that was threatening to break loose.

She didn't give him that moment. She simply looked at him, her eyes wide and soft and shimmering green, and he was lost. And when he reached for her, despite his best efforts not to, she came to him willingly.

He'd half convinced himself he'd imagined it, the fierce, hot sweetness of her mouth, her kiss. He'd told himself it was the long months of celibacy that had done him in, blowing his memory of it out of all proportion with reality; nothing could really feel the way his silly imagination thought that kiss had felt.

He'd been wrong.

Her lips were as soft, her mouth was as honey-sweet, as he remembered. And the flames that leaped to life in him made the fire on the hearth seem like a mere flicker.

He tasted her, long and deep, and she welcomed it, her hands slipping up behind his neck, the slender fingers of one hand threading through his hair. He felt the brush of her touch against his skin, and as if all his nerve endings had awakened at once, he felt the ripple of sensation chase down his back. She made a tiny sound deep in her throat, a low, husky sound that sent a shiver down his spine and hardened him achingly in one pulsing beat of his heart.

He groaned, and tried to pull back, knowing he was careening out of control already. Mercy protested with a tightening of her hands at the back of his neck, and a pressing of her body to his. She moved her mouth coaxingly on his, and then traced his lips with the tip of her tongue. The groan that escaped him then was a long, heartfelt one of pure pleasure.

She seemed to take it as encouragement, and Grant

nearly gasped aloud as she probed past his lips to trace the even ridge of his teeth. He froze, lips still parted, worried beyond reason that she would go no further if he scared her off with his eagerness. Then, gently, he flicked her tongue with his own and drew back in silent invitation. And groaned again when she accepted and tasted him deeply, as if she'd only been waiting for that.

Her eagerness unleashed his own, and his hands slid up to cup her head and hold her steady for his plunging kiss. The shift of his weight overbalanced them, and they slipped down to the cushions of the couch. The feel of her stretched out half beside, half beneath him nearly drove Grant wild, and he couldn't stop himself sliding one hand down her straight, slender back to press her tighter against him.

Her hands shifted, and he felt her fingers digging into the muscles of his shoulders with that strength that had always amazed him. But she wasn't pushing him away, she was urging him on, and when she nipped ever so gently at his lower lip, his hips jerked involuntarily, nudging her thigh with flesh he couldn't ever remember being this hard before.

He didn't know if the room was starting to spin because of the kiss, or because he'd forgotten to breathe. It came down to the same thing in the end, he supposed. Reluctantly he wrenched his mouth away, and for a long moment simply looked down into her wide eyes. They were full of a wonder unlike anything he'd ever seen before, and the thought that he'd put that look there made him feel things he'd never felt before.

He'd never seen her look so thoroughly beguiled,

so completely unshadowed by anything except the fierce need that had so surprisingly captured them both. This was how she should look all the time, he thought. Rid of that hovering sadness, rid of the pain, the dark memories...

God, what was he doing? She'd come here to heal, to mend, before going back to relive the horror of what had happened when the killer was caught and she had to testify about the death of the man she'd loved and respected.

He forced himself to sit up. His body shuddered in protest; it cared nothing about reasons or right or wrong, it cared only that it was being denied when it wanted to seek the haven of her sweet heat more than it wanted to keep breathing. His jaw clenched as he fought himself, as he fought this consuming tide of need he'd never expected to feel in his life, and certainly never expected to feel for this woman.

"Grant?"

Her voice was tentative, quiet, and hovering too close to the edge of hurt for him to miss the undertone.

"Mercy, listen—" he had to stop for a ragged breath "—we have to...stop. I know you're still...off balance a bit here, after Nick—"

She sat up slowly, her breathing as ragged as his own. She looked at him, her lips parted, and still looking slightly swollen from the intensity of their kiss. When she spoke at last, it was with great care. "I know I am."

"So we'd better stop this while...we can."

"But that has nothing to do with this."

"But it does." He was beginning to sound a little

desperate, as his body heard only the acquiescence in her voice, and not the ramifications of what it so badly wanted to do. "They say that, don't they, that when someone close to you...dies, the instinct is to..."

"Sex as affirmation of life, is that what you're saying?"

Grant winced. "It sounds...cold like that, but... sort of, yes."

She stood up, drawing her five-foot-two-inch frame up to its full length, and managing in the process to exude a dignity far beyond her diminutive stature.

"I think you're underestimating yourself and your appeal, Grant. That's rather refreshing, actually. And I even appreciate your effort at...nobility, I suppose. I was a little fragile when I got here, but...not anymore. I've found peace here. And for a moment, I thought I'd found something else, as well."

"I'm not noble," he growled, wondering why, of all she had said, that was what grated on him. Perhaps because he wasn't feeling noble at all right now. He was feeling frustrated, and it was his own stupid fault, for letting his scruples about taking advantage of her vulnerability interfere.

"I understand, Grant. Really. It's common enough, I suppose. But do you really think that I only wanted this because Nick died? To prove to myself that I'm still alive? If you did, you're also underestimating me. This isn't about reaffirming life, or survivor's guilt, or any of the other catchphrases they throw around."

"Mercy—"

"I'm not the child I once was, who thought the sun rose and set in you. It's not about that, either. It's about the simple fact that you make me feel like no man ever has before. And that you admitted...it went both ways. That's all.''

She walked away from him then, her back ramrod-straight, her head high. And he wondered if he'd done more damage than good with all his self-sacrifice here tonight. There were times, he thought with a ruefulness that was almost painful in its strength, when he wished his mother hadn't raised him to be quite so...straight-arrow. When he wished he could do as so many others seemed to, just take the gifts that were handed to them and never question whether the taking would be right or wrong, never taking into account anyone else's feelings in the matter.

But Barbara Jackson McClure Fortune had been a powerful influence on his life—never mind that she'd only been in it part of the time since he'd turned four. Perhaps that was even why her influence had been so powerful; as a child, he'd had so little time with her he was eager to show her he could be the son she wanted him to be. And by the time he realized all his efforts weren't going to put his family back together, he'd already been in the habit.

He let his head loll back on the couch and released a disgusted sigh as he tried to will his still-aroused body into submission.

He heard a short, sharp sound that seemed to echo his own disgust, and looked up to see Gambler on his feet, looking at him with every evidence of wry pity. Once the dog saw that he had Grant's attention, he trotted over to the door.

"That bad, huh?" he muttered as he got up to let

the animal out. "Can't even stand to be in here with me?"

The feisty little shepherd looked back over his shoulder at him, but politely refrained from any further observations as he trotted outside.

Grant closed the door after him, knowing the dog would sleep in the barn as usual; Gambler wasn't a house dog, and had only taken to visiting indoors at all since Mercy had arrived. His dog, his horse, his hands, she'd charmed them all. He couldn't say effortlessly—she'd worked far too hard around here to say that—but she'd certainly done it swiftly enough.

As for what she'd done to him, he wasn't sure he knew the word for that. He wasn't sure there was a word for it.

It was a very long time before he made the lonely trek upstairs.

"Fine way to spend Christmas Eve," he muttered as he strode past her door, jaw clenched, thinking that if he wasn't still so damned horny it was putting his teeth on edge, he'd probably be feeling pretty damn sorry for himself.

She hadn't expected to sleep at all, not after that kiss, so Mercy was startled when the trumpeting bark brought her fully awake in an instant. She'd heard Gambler bark before, when chivying along recalcitrant cattle, when answering a whistle, when alerting them that some unfamiliar and perhaps unfriendly creature was too close to the Aussie dog's turf, when greeting a guest arriving through the front gate. The tough little animal conveyed an amazing amount simply by his tone and the rapidity of the sounds. She'd heard them all, and none of them had ever sounded like this. There was a note to the dog's quick barks that was urgent and worried at the same time, and it made the skin between her shoulder blades prickle.

Without hesitation, she scrambled out of bed and dressed hastily, tugging on her sheepskin boots as she hopped to her door. She heard heavier steps on the stairs just as she pulled the door open, and knew Grant was up and answering Gambler's unmistakable summons.

By the time she got downstairs, he was already outside. She pulled the door open in time to see him running across the yard, the dog, silent now that his call had been answered, leading the way toward the barn.

She carefully closed the door behind her and hurried after them. Her heart jammed upward in her chest when she saw dog and man bypass the main barn and continue on to the smaller barn where the mares were housed.

She knew before she got there, with an instinct she didn't question, that it was Lady, the leopard Appy mare. The moment she stepped into the barn, she heard a harsh, rasping sound, and saw Gambler sitting anxiously before the horse's stall. Grant was just now opening the stall door, having obviously stopped to grab the battery-powered lamp he now held. She ran across the aisle of the barn, wincing at the labored sound of the mare's breathing.

The beautiful mare was down, her distended belly looking even more swollen as she lay on her side. She was sweating, wet with it at neck and flanks. She thrashed briefly, her legs and head flailing. Then she fell back, as if exhausted, her eyes looking dull and flat with weariness. Mercy felt something twist inside her painfully. She watched as Grant checked the horse, laying a gentle hand on her lower belly as he spoke softly to the distressed animal.

"Easy, girl. It's going to be okay. That little one of yours just decided to be a little early. It'll be a Christmas baby, that's all. Easy, now."

It was a tender, almost crooning litany, and the horse seemed to respond, not fighting his touch, but watching him with liquid brown eyes that seemed to understand. Mercy knew this was early. Walt had explained to her that they tried to time breedings on the ranch so that the birth came as soon after the New Year as possible, to give the horse a head start, since for registration and competitive purposes, all horses' birthdays were calculated as January 1.

"Is this early enough to be a problem?"

Grant looked up at her. His eyes widened a fraction, and Mercy became suddenly aware that in her haste she'd left her hair down and not bothered with a bra. But he said nothing, only answered her question.

"Not like that. Doc said she should foal about mid-January, so this is only three weeks early. That's not the problem. There's something else wrong."

"Something else?"

"Normally, a mare foals within a half an hour of her water bag breaking. She did it in fifteen minutes, last time. But it looks like she's been down for a while. If the foal started before things went wrong, if it's in the passage or the cord is twisted, it could die."

Mercy stared, her stomach knotting. "Do you want me to call someone? A vet?"

Grant shook his head grimly. "It'd take Doc Watson two hours to get here, even if we could find him on Christmas Eve. I don't think the foal has that kind of time. And she may not, either. She's exhausted."

Mercy's eyes widened. She'd grown quite fond of the gentle, pretty mare, feeding her bits of carrots and apples while she sympathized with her ungainliness.

"She's not going to die, is she?"

"Not if I can help it," Grant said.

"What can I do to help?"

He glanced up at her. "Ever delivered a baby, Officer Brady?"

"Once," she said.

"Get ready for your second, then."

If he meant to intimidate her, he failed. "Will you need the traditional hot water?" she asked mildly.

A grin flickered across his face. "Absolutely."

"I'll get back to the house."

The grin widened. "Just the tap over there will do. It comes out really hot. Almost boiling, in fact. I'll wash up there. That's why we put that little hot-water heater and sink out here."

"Oh." She couldn't help smiling back. "Clever."

"Walt's idea. Nothing's too good for his mares. He's had that heater turned on for a couple of days now, and moved her into this foaling stall last week. He must have suspected she was going to pull this on us."

Mercy looked around at the stall, which was larger than the others, almost twelve foot square. The hayrack that was low on the wall of the other stalls was missing, she supposed for safety's sake.

"I wish *he* was here to help you," she said fervently.

"You'll do fine, Mercy." He began to give a string of orders, but Mercy didn't quibble; he knew what to do, and she didn't. "Get me that blue box out of the tack cabinet over there, and the clean towels that are there. I'll need that heat lamp, too. Plug it into the light fixture outside the door. I'll need it to warm the towels, and it's cold enough the foal may need help drying off. And get that lantern like this one from the other barn, will you? Those overhead lights in the breezeway aren't going to be enough. I don't want to hurt her because I can't see."

"All right."

She got the box, heat lamp and towels for him first, then hurried over to the other barn. Joker whinnied as she came in, but she spared him only a pat on the nose as she went by his stall. He protested as she grabbed the lantern and headed back at a run, but she hushed him rather vehemently.

"You be quiet," she ordered. "It's your baby she's trying to deliver, and the least you can do is shut up while she's doing it."

She never stopped moving, and she was out the door on her last word. Surprisingly—or perhaps not— the big stallion made no further noise.

When she got back, Grant was kneeling beside the still-downed horse. He had discarded his heavy jacket and already washed up; she could see damp spots on the edges of the sleeves of his utilitarian gray T-shirt, indicating that he'd scrubbed his arms almost to his shoulders.

Well, it should have been utilitarian. On Grant it looked...amazing. Stretched across his broad chest, snug around his muscular arms and tucked into his jeans over his flat, fit belly, it reminded her rather forcefully that she rarely saw him like this, and inspired a wayward wish to come back to the ranch in warm weather, to see him regularly without heavy winter gear.

"Set that lantern over there and turn it on," he instructed her. She did so, and the beam of light lit up the rest of the stall. "I've got to check on what's wrong inside. Pray I don't find feet bottoms up."

"What does that mean?"

"It means they're probably the hind feet, and we've got a bigger problem than I can handle. Try and keep her calm, will you? She's pretty tired, but she might kick me anyway for what I'm about to do."

Mercy saw him kneel behind the horse, and when she realized how he meant to check on the foal, literally by feel, she winced.

"I certainly would," she muttered under her breath as she dropped to her knees beside the mare's head. Not sure what to do, she simply began to stroke the mare's sweat-dampened neck, and to talk. She adopted the same tone she used with Joker, a crooning sort of teasing, saying whatever came to mind, but always in that same soothing voice.

"Of course, he's just a man, what does he know about it, right, honey? But he's going to help you, really he is, and your baby, and everything will be just fine, sweetie, you just hang on..."

It was taking forever. She couldn't look at Grant, couldn't bear to see what he was doing. The mare flailed once, and she heard him bite out a short curse, and wondered if one of the hooves had caught him. But he didn't move away, and she just continued to pet and croon to the animal.

At last she heard him let out a grunt of satisfaction. She gave the mare a final pat, and then looked up at him; he was wiping off his arm and looking rather pleased.

"Okay, girl, it's up to you now."

"What was it? It wasn't backward?"

"No. Just a foreleg bent back. Should be okay now—I think I got it in the right position." He reached over and flipped the extra lantern off, then got up and did the same with the other. When she looked at him questioningly, he explained, "The foal won't like that bright light."

Before he even finished the words, it had begun. The mare, as if revitalized by the realization that her pushing was no longer futile, gave several small grunts. A membrane-covered shape began to emerge. Mercy held her breath. It wasn't clean, it wasn't tidy, but it was a miracle nevertheless. In what seemed like no time at all, the tiny creature—all legs, it seemed— was sprawled on the straw. The living image of its father, dramatic white blanket and all.

Grant moved swiftly but without haste, to avoid startling either the weary mother or the equally weary newborn. With the remaining clean towels he had warmed with the lamp, he wiped down the foal, standing under the heat lamp's glow. She watched as he gently, almost tenderly, handled the tiny horse, attending to the umbilical cord, then carefully lifting the foal and setting it down near the mare's head. Exhausted as she was, the mare nuzzled her baby.

"Take it easy, Mama," Grant whispered. "She's here, and okay, and you both need to rest. You had a tough time."

"Is it?" Mercy asked softly. "A she?" She hadn't been close enough to tell in the faint light.

Grant glanced at her and grinned. But his voice was equally soft as he told her, "It is. She's going to be the prettiest filly in the county, with her mama's conformation and her daddy's coat."

She smiled back at him, feeling almost deliriously happy, and a little embarrassed at the fierceness of her response to this event, and the sight of the little horse, the new life that had not been here before. New life. The cycle continuing. Life and death and life... And she knew in that instant that she was going to be all right. That although she would never forget Nick, would never cease feeling his loss, she would go on. She would find joy and pleasure in life again, somehow, sometime. She might be as shaky as this newborn foal, but she would survive. As Nick would have wanted her to survive.

A little dazed by this revelation, Mercy stayed silent, watching. She'd thought it was over, but she found she'd been vastly mistaken. There was, apparently, still much work to do. Grant swiftly and efficiently cleaned up the soiled bedding, disposed of the afterbirth, and in between gave the mare sips of lukewarm water. Then he tossed down a small amount of alfalfa hay for her. This took some time, and by the time he was done, the mare had gotten to her feet.

He seemed to relax a little at this, but he kept moving, gently washing the mare's udder in preparation for the foal's first effort at nursing.

At last he stepped outside the stall and closed the door, saying rest and quiet were the best things for mother and baby now. But he stayed, watching carefully from outside, and Mercy could see from his expression that he was still concerned for the animals, after the delayed birth. The minutes ticked by, until Mercy guessed at least an hour had passed since the foal had been born.

Gambler, who had been sitting quietly out of the way, now came over and sat at their feet.

"Good boy," Grant murmured, reaching down to tickle the dog's ears, but still never taking his eyes off the occupants of the stall.

"More than that," Mercy said, dropping down beside the shepherd and looking into the blue and brown eyes. "You were wonderful."

Gambler gave a low whine, as if mindful of the need for quiet. But it was unmistakably a welcoming sound, and Mercy risked a quick rub behind the dog's ears. He allowed it, as if even he felt the specialness of the occasion.

"Mercy."

She straightened at the sound of Grant's voice, wondering at the pleased undertone. He wasn't looking at her, he was staring into the stall. She looked. In time to see the foal, her tiny hooves spread far apart for balance, wobbling on her ungainly, spindly legs. But she was up.

Then she went down in a heap. Mercy made a sound of dismay, but Grant put a hand on her arm in reassurance. And even as he did, the foal struggled up again, and this time managed to stay upright.

"Good," Grant said in satisfaction. "She was only tired after the birth. Nothing seems to be wrong. Now if she can just find breakfast..."

It took the ungainly baby a few tries, but with some softly whickered encouragement from the mare, the foal found her way and was soon nursing hungrily. This last hurdle overcome, Mercy felt the tension flow out of Grant as if it were a tangible thing.

She glanced at his face. He was smiling, a soft, pleased, quiet kind of smile. And something about it made her go quivery inside. Twelve years ago, Kristina had always teased her when she said she didn't like Grant just because he was good-looking, that she liked what he was on the inside, as well as the outside. Her friend hadn't believed it, but Mercy knew that it was this Grant, the Grant who really cared, that she had sensed was there even then.

Mercy looked at them—mother, baby, man and dog. Grant glanced at her. Something in her expression made him stare. And then, blinking rapidly, she turned and ran out of the barn before the tears began to flow down her cheeks.

Grant McClure, she thought, was an amazing man.

And this was the most beautiful Christmas Eve she'd ever spent.

Ten

"Any of that brandy-laced fruit juice left?"

The call came from the living room. She wasn't really surprised; Grant should be tired, after the interruption to his sleep, but then, so should she, and she didn't feel the slightest bit sleepy. Not after the small miracle of life they'd witnessed tonight.

"I'm heating it up now," she called, and added teasingly, "You weren't kidding about long showers. I was afraid I was going to have to come see if you were still alive in there."

"I wish you had."

His voice was low, husky, heart-stoppingly suggestive—and very, very close. Mercy jumped, startled that once again he'd managed to get so close without her knowing. She was getting rusty; too relaxed, that was what it was. All her well-trained instincts were being lulled by this peaceful place—

And then all thought fled as she turned around. He was barely two feet away, and clad only in a low-slung pair of jeans. A towel was slung around his neck, and his hair was still wet, slicked back from his face and making the rugged squareness of his jaw even more apparent. His bare feet explained the lack of warning footsteps. But nothing could explain the way her heart began to hammer at the sight of his bare chest and belly, the way her eyes drank in the lean, solid muscles of his arms. Nothing except the explanation she was afraid to accept, that Grant Mc-Clure was now and always had been the only man ever to truly move her. In all the ways a woman wanted, needed, to be moved.

And the idea that she'd somehow sensed that even at twelve was nothing less than frightening.

I wish you had....

His softly spoken, unmistakably sensual words echoed in her head, and the images they evoked took her breath away.

As if he'd read her thoughts, as if he knew she'd just played back his words in her head, he stepped closer, cornering her against the counter, and added in an even softer, more provocative tone, "You could have joined me."

She gasped. Her eyes widened, and she knew she was staring at him, but she couldn't help herself. She'd never done such a thing, but somehow her imagination was supplying vivid—and erotic—visions of her slipping naked into the shower with Grant. Of how he would look, water streaming over the taut planes and hollows of his body, of how his skin, slick with wetness, would feel beneath her hands.

As if the images had become tactile, as well as visual, her hands curled, her nails digging into her palms, to ease the sudden itch she felt, the sudden need to touch him. It was all she could do not to lift her hands and press them against his chest, the chest that was so very close, so close she could feel the heat of him reaching her in waves. She knew what he would feel like, heavy satin stretched over tensile muscles, and the knowledge only made it harder for her to keep from reaching to do it. But he'd pulled away from her before, and she didn't know if she could deal with him doing it again.

"And if you keep looking at me like that," he said gruffly, "we're going to be right back where we were last night."

Her breath caught. "But…"

"Have you changed your mind?" he asked, a little abruptly.

It would end, here and now, if she said yes. She knew that, knew it deep down in that part of her soul where she kept the few things left in her life that she trusted utterly. Her faith in her own courage had once been kept there, as well; she didn't know where it was now. But no matter her loss of faith in herself, she had never lost faith in Grant's honor; he would never, ever force himself on or seduce a hesitant woman. Even if he knew he could overcome her reservations with just one more searing, burning kiss.

But if she said she'd changed her mind, it would be a lie. And a cowardly one, at that.

"I… You're the one who…stopped," she reminded him, then wondered what on earth she was doing, provoking him, when she should be scurrying for the safety of her room. Although closing the door on the man wouldn't close the door on the feelings he roused in her. No door, real or imagined, was strong enough or solid enough to do that.

"I stopped last night because I thought it was for the wrong reasons. Because you needed to…throw

life back in death's face," he said. "I didn't want you
to…regret it later."

"Then why—?"

"Because now," he said, in that same soft, husky
voice that made her shiver, "I think you want to celebrate life."

He took that last half step, and she felt the press
of his solid, strong body against hers. She shivered,
which made no sense to her, since he was so impossibly, incredibly warm.

"I saw your face in the barn, Mercy," he sad.
"You really felt the miracle, didn't you? New life,
replacing old, the circle unbroken…animals or people, it's the same. It goes on. And you'll go on. You
realized that tonight, didn't you?"

She supposed she should startled by his perception,
but she wasn't. It didn't seem at all odd to her that
this man had seemingly read perfectly the revelation
that had left her more than a little dazed.

"Yes," she said, her voice low and quiet. "I'll
never stop missing Nick, but I'll go on. I owe him
that much. I'll go on. And it will be worth it."

"You'll do more than go on, Mercy. You'll be
happy again. You'll go back to your work, and you'll
find satisfaction in it again. You'll heal, Mercy. There
will always be the scar, but it will never, ever hurt
you as much again."

"Celebrate life…" She whispered the words he'd
said, as if they were a prayer. As, perhaps, they were.

"Yes," Grant said. "And that's the best reason I
can think of for this."

She knew in the instant before he moved that he
was going to kiss her. And almost as quickly, her

body reacted, as if it had known this man's kisses for years. At the same time, she felt as if all the fantasizing she'd done as that infatuated child had been a poor prelude to the sizzling, powerful reality. Nothing in her life had ever prepared her for the feel of his mouth on hers, for the heat generated in her by his coaxing lips, for the powerful jolt that shot through her when his tongue swept past her parted lips and darted into her mouth, tasting, teasing, tempting.

Nothing ever could have prepared her; she couldn't be prepared for something she hadn't known was possible. She'd thought herself more familiar than most with her own body and its reactions; she'd had to work it to peak physical condition, she'd pushed it to almost every limit there was, she'd put it under incredible stress, both physical and mental, and thought she'd learned her own limits.

Until Grant McClure kissed her, and taught her that in this, there were no limits.

With a growling sound, he wrapped his arms around her and pulled her tight against his bare chest. Her breath left her in a rush at the feel of it, at the solid wall of flesh, at the sleek heat of his skin. She lifted her hands, helplessly, needing to touch him more than she'd ever needed anything in her life. Her fingers slid over the hot satin of his skin, tingled at the roughness of the scattering of hair over his chest.

She brushed over his nipples and heard him suck in a quick breath in the same instant. Her own nipples hardened in reaction as an image of him doing the same to her flashed through her mind.

Grant deepened the kiss, probing, tasting, and when he withdrew she followed willingly, eagerly, searching the depths of his mouth just as he had hers. She felt a shudder ripple through him as her tongue stroked his, and an echoing convulsion swept her as his hands slid down to her hips and urged her even closer.

Although he made no effort to hide it, it was a moment before she realized the significance of the pressure she was feeling against her belly. Tentatively, barely realizing what she was doing, she shifted her body, pressing against that masculine hardness. Grant stiffened, and his hands clutched at her waist as a throttled groan broke from him. The sound gave her an odd sort of thrill; she'd never thought much about this kind of power before, perhaps because she'd always been so focused on the purely physical power necessary to do her job. Or perhaps because she'd never really wielded this kind of power before, the kind of feminine power that brought a strong man to this kind of desperation.

Grant broke the kiss, and for a moment stood staring down at her, a wildness in his eyes that electrified her, because she knew it was for her.

"Grant," she whispered.

"Tell me," he said hoarsely, his breathing coming in harsh gulps. "Because if we're going to stop...it has to be now."

One last, tiny reservation nagged at her. "I'm still a city girl, Grant. And you don't like them much."

"I know. And I know you'll go back. But city girl or not, you're a diamond, Mercy. Pure and clear and flawless."

She was hardly that, but this didn't seem the moment to correct him.

"A man doesn't often get a chance to hold a diamond like that," he said. "But when he does... nothing else matters."

He kissed her again, deeply, thoroughly, until her skin tingled and her every sense soared. She was so lost in the new sensations that she was only vaguely aware of it when he lifted her in his arms, noticing that he was carrying her only when he turned sideways to get through the kitchen doorway.

"Grant?"

He looked for an instant as if he feared she'd changed her mind, and as if he were considering kissing her again before she could say so. But after a moment he merely said, "What?"

"I...I'm not...on anything. Pills, I mean."

It took a moment for it to register. Then his mouth quirked. "I've got something." She blinked, and Grant smiled wryly. "When Rita asked me to make sure Chipper knew about condoms, I never figured I'd be using the visual aids."

Mercy giggled. And looked startled at the sound of it; she was not, by any stretch of the imagination, a giggling kind of woman. Grant looked as surprised as she felt, but then he grinned at her, and bent to kiss her again. By the time they reached the top of the stairs, the only thing she could think of to say was "Hurry."

Heat blazed in Grant's eyes at the word, or at the urgency in her tone—she supposed it didn't matter which. As long as he did as she asked. And he did; despite carrying her, he took the stairs two at a time.

And then stopped dead, in front of the door to the room she'd been using.

"Your place or mine?"

Mercy shifted a little, leaning back in his arms to look up at him quizzically. "Does it…matter?"

"It seems to," he answered, a little sheepishly. "I've never…done this here." His mouth twisted wryly. "I haven't done it at all for…longer than I can remember right now."

"Neither have I," she whispered as pleasure at his words flooded through her.

I've never done this here. A simple thing, yet it made her feel incredibly special. And truly wanted, beyond the urgent physical need that was possessing both of them. Foolish, perhaps, but she couldn't deny it.

"Yours," she said abruptly.

Grant took in a deep breath; she felt the rise of his broad chest. His eyes closed for a moment, and he swallowed tightly. Then he opened them and, looking down at her, nodded once, almost sharply. But what she saw in his face belied the silence of his reaction.

"Right answer?" she asked, feeling suddenly nervous.

"Yes." His voice was low, rough. "I want you in my bed. And if that's not delicate enough or sensitive enough, I'm sorry."

"Don't apologize," Mercy managed to say, with what little breath his words had left her.

He strode off down the hall, still carrying her as if she were no more burden than the tiny foal had been. He thought he wasn't sensitive enough? Had he forgotten that she'd watched him handle that tiny creature as if it were the most fragile thing on the planet? That she'd seen him soothe that frightened, exhausted mare with a voice and touch as delicate as any she'd ever known? Had he truly not realized how much of himself he'd shown her tonight?

She had no time to dwell on the thought; Grant pushed the door to his room open with his bare foot, and carried her inside. She had never been in here, had only glanced in once or twice when he left the door open, enough to know that the room was quietly masculine, with solid, heavy furniture and deep colors. The bedclothes, simple white sheets and plain blankets topped with a dark blue quilt, were tossed to one side, where they'd landed when he rolled out at Gambler's alarm. A shirt was tossed over the foot of the bed, and a pocket watch lay next to a comb on the dresser. But it was the stack of at least a half-dozen books that sat on the nightstand that made Mercy smile; in the view of a lot of the world, Grant might have chosen to "waste himself" out here, but he'd never stopped working his excellent mind.

He set her down beside the bed, letting her slide down his body slowly, intimately, as if he wanted to feel every inch of her with every inch of himself. The idea made her shiver with renewed need. He felt it, she knew he did, because his eyes widened, then narrowed, and she knew she'd never before seen a heat like the heat that flashed in that vivid blue.

He kissed her again, even more fiercely this time, hungrily, as if she were the first taste of spring after a Wyoming mountain winter. She sagged against him, wondering where all her finely honed strength had vanished to. With a low, almost primitive sound that was somehow undeniably and vehemently male, he eased her down onto the bed. She thought he would follow, but instead he turned and yanked open the nightstand drawer with far more force than was probably necessary. He fumbled in the drawer for a moment, making her wonder if possibly, just possibly, he might be shaking just as she was.

Her eyes automatically followed the movement as he tossed a foil packet on top of the nightstand. Her gaze flicked to his face. He grimaced.

"I don't trust myself to remember it...later."

That simple statement, and all it implied, sent a shudder through Mercy. He came down beside her in a rush, grabbing her swiftly, the urgent need in his face taking away any sense of unease. He kissed her again, brow, cheeks, chin, the tip of her nose, then rained a fiery path of nibbling kisses down the side of her throat.

He tugged at the hem of the sweatshirt she'd pulled on in such a rush. Mercy shifted to oblige him, freeing her arms from the sleeves herself, remembering only when he moved to pull the soft, well-worn shirt over her head that she wore no bra. In the moment Grant freed her from the shirt, she heard him groan. And then she felt his hands on her breasts, cupping them almost reverently. She felt each of his fingers like a brand, searing her, making her nipples draw up tight and hard.

She looked down, and the contrast of his tanned, finely muscled and work-strengthened hands against the soft white flesh of her breasts made her shiver. He paused, glancing at her as if he were unsure she welcomed his touch. She opened her mouth to speak, to beg, if necessary, if that was what it would take to get him to move his fingers that crucial distance to the taut peaks that had turned from pale pink to deep rose. But she was beyond words, and so told him in the only way she could think of; she arched her back, thrusting her breasts upward to him.

He muttered something low and harsh and dark-sounding that she didn't quite hear. And then she didn't care; he caught her nipples between his fingers and gently plucked them to exquisite hardness. Mercy cried out, stiffening in shock as arrows of fire shot from that aroused flesh. Heat seemed to erupt in her then, careening around until it settled low inside her.

Her cry seemed to galvanize him, and he made swift work of her jeans and her soft sheepskin boots. For a moment, he simply looked at her, and had it not been for the raw desire that tightened his face into taut planes, she might have been embarrassed.

"Mercy," Grant whispered, then kissed her again. "Who'd have thought that little imp would grow up so beautifully?"

"You were always beautiful, to me," she whispered, recovering her voice at last.

Grant flushed slightly. "You were...prejudiced."

"Yes. I still am. Even overdressed, you're beautiful."

He took her hint, and skinned out of his jeans. When he turned back to her, Mercy took her own long, lingering look. He let her, as if in return for his own slow stare at her. She'd known he was strong, solid, and utterly male, but this sight of his naked body made her imaginings pale by comparison. His chest seemed even broader when she could see the way it narrowed to his trim waist and flat, ridged belly. The source of his easy grace was obvious to her now, with the sight of his slim hips, strong legs, and high taut backside; riding did work some interesting muscles, she thought.

And the tight jeans that she'd thought did little to conceal the contours of that most masculine part of him in fact had concealed a great deal; he was as strong and powerful there as everywhere else. And if she'd had any doubts left about the genuineness of his need, they were gone now, dispelled by the sight of his fierce arousal. She trembled, half in anticipation, half in apprehension, of what was to come.

Her thoughts must have been clear on her face, because Grant's brow furrowed. "Mercy?"

"I..."

She saw his jaw tighten, but he asked evenly enough, "Do you want to stop?"

"No," she said quickly, "it's not that, it's just... it's been a long time, and you're..."

"I'm what?

"In proportion," she said, blushing furiously.

"Oh." He looked as if he were pleased, but wasn't sure if he should show it or not. "Is that... Are you..." He stopped, blushing himself this time. "I didn't really think about how little you are."

"I'm not little," she protested automatically. "You're just..."

Her voice trailed away as she looked him up and down again. And she completely forgot what she'd been going to say. She could only stare, the thought of him making love to her with that splendid body making her quiver, inside and out. She heard Grant smother what sounded like a gasp, as if he'd been kicked in the belly.

"Later," he said, grating the words out, "later I want to look at you like you're looking at me now, for a long, long time. I want you to touch everything you're looking at, and I want to do the same to you. But later. Please."

He reached for her then, and she rolled into his embrace eagerly. His hands seemed everywhere, stroking, caressing, seeking and finding every nerve ending in a body awakening to this kind of sweetness like never before.

She felt herself moving, shifting restlessly on the bed, and for the first time in her life she felt utterly out of control of her body. It was Grant's to command, and he did so with every lingering touch, and she couldn't find it in her to care. She didn't care about anything except his not stopping until this awful, wonderful pressure building within her eased, until he gave her what she needed, what only he could give, to sear away this aching, pulsing need.

When his hand gently probed between her legs, she knew what he would find, felt her own heat and dampness before his fingers proved it with their easy slide over feminine flesh slick with its own wetness.

Her breath caught and she moaned his name when he found and teased that tiny knot of nerve endings he'd so thoroughly brought to attention. She grabbed his shoulders, clutching at him, thinking he was the only stable thing in a world that was threatening to spin out of its orbit.

Never ceasing that maddening circling caress, he took her hand in his free one and dragged it down his body. She hesitated, feeling suddenly shy. In her five years as a cop, she'd seen, by necessity, her share of things sexual. But that was different, this was Grant, and this was pure and clean and good and so far removed from the garbage she dealt with in her work that she felt utterly naive.

"I don't know..." she began, letting her voice trail away when she realized how silly it sounded, pleading ignorance at her age and with her background.

But Grant didn't seem to find anything silly about it. "Ah, Mercy, sweetheart...I'll show you."

The unexpected endearment made her pulse leap. It began to pound in her ears as he guided her hand, curling her fingers around him, showing her the motion, the degree of tightness. She stroked him, once, then twice, and he pulled his hand away. She did it again, and reveled in his groan of undisguised pleasure. Base to sensitive tip, she caressed him, tiny frissons of heated sensation shooting through her at the feel of that hard, silken-smooth and fire-hot flesh beneath her fingers. At the same time, his own fingers were driving her to the brink of madness, making her burn with a heat she'd never known, even as she wanted to cry out from the unbearable hollowness she was feeling, an emptiness only he could fill.

In the same instant she knew she could bear it no more, Grant's hips bucked, pushing him hard against her hand.

"All night," he told her, his voice a harsh rasp. "I swear, next time we'll do this all night, Mercy. And we'll do it any way you want, anywhere you want. But I can't wait anymore."

Swiftly he opened the foil packet he'd set out. When he finally shifted over her, she welcomed him, parting her legs to cradle him as her arms wrapped around him.

"Yes," she whispered, as she felt the first probing touch of blunt male flesh, "Oh, yes, Grant, now."

He slid into her in one easy motion, as if their bodies had only been waiting for this moment to show them how perfectly they fit together. Grant froze, then shuddered at the moment he was in her to the hilt, and Mercy cried out his name at the wonderful fullness of it.

Grant said something under his breath, a passionate growling of her name and a wondering, slightly awestruck oath. She felt him shudder again, and pulled him closer, tighter. She hadn't known enough to imagine this kind of closeness in the childhood days when she was so absorbed by her crush on him. If she had, she thought now, as he began to slowly move, to draw back and then renew the deep, hot pleasure by pushing into her again and again, she would never have recovered from it.

If, indeed, she ever had.

But it didn't matter now. Nothing mattered, except that this was Grant the man, not the boy, and he was teaching her things she'd never known, with the driving power of his body and the fierce glow of pure, hot desire in his eyes. With each motion of his hips he drove her higher, until she was rising to meet him eagerly, wantonly, until the room echoed with the sound of flesh against flesh, and the covers that were meant to protect against the winter cold were kicked aside, unnecessary in the face of the heat they were generating.

Grant swore softly, reverently, then said her name

in a voice she would never forget. His hand slipped between them, to find and stroke that bit of flesh yet again. At his first touch, Mercy cried out. Convulsively she arched against him, and he stroked her again, harder, then harder, caressing her with his fingers as his flesh filled her to an exquisite tightness.

She prayed he wouldn't stop, wished she could find the words to beg him not to stop, but nothing seemed able to escape her except a continuous moaning of his name.

And then her body tightened like a drawn bow as the explosion began. Her body clenched around his, making her even more potently aware of his presence inside her. She heard him cry out her name, felt him arch and slam into her one last time, and then she was lost to everything except the convulsive rippling of her body and the sizzling waves of heated sensation that ripped along every nerve.

Only gradually did she come back to herself, becoming aware of Grant's harsh, rapid breathing first. She lay there for a long time, simply savoring the unexpectedly welcome weight of him, treasuring the sheen of sweat on his skin, loving the way he still gripped her shoulders, as he had for his final thrust, tightly, as if he feared she would vanish if he let go. She felt the sudden welling of tears, coming upon her so quickly, as they had that day by the pond, and she couldn't stop them.

And she wondered what new set of problems she'd managed to create for herself. She was here, in Grant's arms—something she'd dreamed about incessantly twelve years ago. But her life was in the city, and his was irrevocably here. And she had little faith in the probability of success for long-distance relationships.

But they would deal with that later. For now, just being here was enough. Just feeling his solid weight was enough.

But she couldn't help wondering if he still hated city girls.

Eleven

He had to stop this. Dreaming about Mercy every night wasn't just going to drive him crazy, it was going to kill him. He'd never awakened so tired so often as he had since she'd arrived on the ranch. Although, he mused sleepily, he didn't feel particularly tired this morning. In fact, he felt pretty damn good, cozy, comfy, warm, relaxed, and amazingly pleased with the world. In a minute he'd try to remember why. But for now he'd stay in this half-asleep place, where everything was wonderful and the lingering effects of the dream had him half convinced it really was Mercy tucked into the curve of his body, her sweet backside warming already warm flesh.

He jerked awake, coming up on one elbow abruptly. The room was bright enough to tell him first that it was much later than his usual rising hour of five, and second that the snow had probably stopped and the sun was out. The third thing the nicely lit room told him was exactly why he was feeling so damn smug.

It all had been real. It hadn't been another of those vivid, erotic dreams. She was here. Mercy was here, in his bed, naked, her slender shoulders bare above the covers, even though the room was a bit chilly, the pale blond silk of her hair spread out around her. Hair that he now knew intimately, as he'd stroked its length, and felt the soft, enticing brush of it all over his body.

It all came back to him in a rush, the memories of last night, of his own fever, and her fiery response to it. The images that flashed through his mind hardened him with a speed that made him gasp. The first time, when he'd realized she was crying, and fear had knotted his gut until her words by the pond had come back to him.

Sometimes, when something...makes me feel so much, it kind of bubbles out...

Want and need and desire had slammed into him again at what she'd silently told him with her tears, about how he'd made her feel. And time after time they had come together, each time more intense, until he'd wondered that either of them could still move. Then they'd both fallen into an exhausted sleep, arms and legs still entangled.

Mercy moved then, murmuring slightly as she snuggled closer. Grant stifled a groan as the taut curves of her buttocks stroked rapidly expanding flesh.

He'd never felt this before, this sense of joy in the morning, this feeling of utter rightness of waking with a woman in his arms. Not just any woman, this woman. He supposed he'd known, when he wanted her here, in the bed he himself had been conceived in, that some part of him knew this was different. That it would be like this.

He fought the urge to give in to it, to savor the unexpected morning sweetness, the pleasure of simply her presence. His heart, his gut and his body might be rejoicing, but his head was sending out warnings as loud as Gambler's bark.

She was still a city girl. She'd said so herself. And she'd as much as told him she would go back to being a city girl.

I promise this will only be for a while. As soon as they call me, I'll be on the next plane out, and out of your way.

She'd said it, in so many words. And he hadn't forgotten it, not really. It just hadn't mattered, not last night, not when he wanted her so fiercely that the logical, rational part of his mind that warned him when he was about to do something stupid seemingly ceased to function.

And now? Now that he knew just what was possible, now that he knew that Mercy reached him in ways no woman ever had, in ways he'd never imagined, even in the most taunting, teasing dreams he ever had?

Now that he knew, had a single damn thing changed?

He felt something tighten deep inside him, something he hadn't felt since Constance had handed him his battered heart back on a platter.

You went into this with your eyes open, he thought grimly. *You knew she would leave.* There was nothing here powerful enough to hold a woman who wasn't born to it. Including him.

Mercy stirred again. He wanted more than anything to kiss her awake, slowly, softly. He wanted to see it in her eyes again, that fire, that passion, wanted her to reach for him again, eagerly, wanted to hear that tiny gasp of pleasure when he slid himself deep into her.

He didn't do any of it. With the sinking emotions of a man who knew he was already in way over his head, he drew away from her. His body protested the loss of her soft warmth, clenching violently. And when she rolled over and her lashes slowly lifted, when he looked down into those sleepy green eyes, it took every bit of determination he had not to grab her and do something even more stupid than he already had, and tell her things he didn't want to say and she didn't want to hear.

"Good morning," she said, and the soft, loving smile that curved her mouth squeezed at his heart.

"Barely," he said, knowing he sounded a little gruff, but unable to help it. The need to stay close warred with the need to pull back to safety, and the result was a tension that was rapidly building to the snapping point inside him.

Mercy blinked. "What time is it?"

"Late," he said, succinct to the point of bluntness.

Her forehead creased as his tone registered through her morning drowsiness. She sat up. His gut knotted as she moved, baring the long, slender lines of her back down to the gentle flare of her hips to his gaze. The images flooded him again, her breasts in his hands, her hips cradling him so sweetly, her hot, slick flesh coaxing him to a climax more powerful than any in his life. He closed his eyes, swallowed tightly, and turned his head away. Only when he was safely facing the window that looked out over the yard did he open his eyes again.

"Grant?"

"I need to go check on the foal," he said, rather abruptly, and sat up himself.

"Is something wrong?"

He swung his feet over the side of the bed and reached for the jeans he'd discarded so hastily last night.

"If I'm supposed to be reading your mind," she said quietly, "I'm afraid I'm not doing very well."

He twisted around to look at her. She had clutched the covers in front of herself, hiding the body she'd given him so freely last night. Her eyes were wide and troubled, but she was looking at him steadily. Facing this as she faced everything—head-on. He owed her at least that much in turn, he thought. Just because he'd found so much more than he ever expected to, that was no reason to change the rules now. At least she'd been honest from the beginning; she'd never led him to believe anything other than that she would go straight back to the city as soon as she could.

"It's all right, Mercy," he said. "I know that last night didn't...change anything." Her eyes widened further, and he hurried to get it all out. "You'll still go back to where you belong. And I'll stay here where I belong."

"I...see."

He couldn't read her tone, couldn't decipher the odd look that had come across her face. Doubt suddenly assailed him. In his effort to make things easier, had he somehow done the opposite?

"We knew that all the time, right? You have your world, I have mine, and they don't meet or mix."

"So you've said."

She sounded a little stiff, and he wasn't sure why. He was only trying to reassure her that he didn't expect anything more than what they both knew would happen. What they'd found together had been...incredible, but it didn't change the basic facts, that he couldn't live in her world and she couldn't live in his.

"Mercy—"

"We'd better get going," she said. "The ranch doesn't know it's a holiday, isn't that what you said?"

Something was wrong, he could feel it, but her expression was utterly neutral. She was reaching for her own clothes, and she had the sweatshirt pulled on before he could think of another word to say.

He was barely into his own jeans when she stood up and turned to face him.

"So," she said brightly, so brightly he wondered if it was for real, "let's go check on the new arrival. Is it all right to take Mom an apple?"

He blinked, taken aback by her sudden cheer. "A piece of one, no more. Mercy, listen, if I said something—"

"Forget it, country boy."

He wondered if the words were a jab, but she said them so cheerfully it didn't seem possible. Then she headed for the door. She stopped as she pulled it open, and looked back over her shoulder at him.

"I'll say one thing, McClure. You sure know how to show a city girl a memorable morning after."

And then she was gone, and Grant found himself unable to move until long after the echo of her footsteps faded away down the hall.

* * *

It would be easier, Mercy thought as she hunched into her jacket and tried not to shiver, if she could write the whole thing off as a mistake. But how could she? How could what had happened between them be a mistake? She might not have had much experience, but she wasn't so naive that she believed everyone found such pleasure.

Or perhaps they did; perhaps she was that naive. Perhaps it had been nothing special, at least to Grant. How else could he have said what he'd said?

You'll still go back to where you belong. And I'll stay here where I belong. You have your world, I have mine, and they don't meet or mix.

And he'd said it so...so reassuringly. As if he expected her to take comfort in the fact that he still expected her to go home. As if he were reminding her that once a city girl, always a city girl, still applied. As if he'd been afraid she would think...think what?

Perhaps that was what his words had been, a warning. A warning she was supposed to heed, a warning that since he apparently expected nothing from her, she should expect nothing from him in turn.

Well, she didn't. She didn't expect a darn thing from Grant McClure, she thought angrily, swiping at eyes that threatened to brim over, adding to her inner tumult. *You're a fool, Brady,* she muttered to herself. You knew this was the way it would be. You said it yourself, before last night, and surely you're not stupid enough to really believe that one night would change it?

But she wasn't going to be one of those weepy

females who claimed to have been led down the garden path. She hadn't been led anywhere, she'd been a willing—more than willing—participant. She was a grown-up, a woman, not a child. She'd made her decision, and now she would live with the results. She had no right to be upset, simply because Grant had voiced what they both already knew. He was just being honest, something she'd always claimed she wanted, so it was rather hypocritical of her to resent it.

At least he didn't know how hurt she'd been by his words. If she'd learned nothing else in five years as a cop, she'd learned how to conceal her emotional reactions. And she wasn't about to let Grant know she really had been foolish enough to think, if only for a moment, that one night together meant anything more than just that. She knew now, in the morning light, that no matter how incredible, how earth-shatteringly passionate, it had been, that it didn't change a thing. And she'd been bright, chipper and, she hoped, convincingly blasé, never mind that it was the hardest thing she'd ever done. If Grant could walk away from what had happened between them, then so could she.

She'd wondered last night if he still hated city girls. She guessed she'd gotten her answer this morning.

A movement on the edge of her vision caught her eye, and she glanced to her right as Gambler trotted toward her. He fell into step beside her as she headed for the mare's barn.

"On your rounds, fella?" she asked.

The little shepherd made a whuffling, satisfied noise that sounded for all the world like an affirmative answer that was also meant to convey that all was well. She glanced down at him; he was looking at her as he went, his parti-colored eyes regarding her steadily.

"How's the baby?"

Gambler gave a short yip, and broke into a lope, headed toward the smaller barn, as if he'd understood perfectly and was deigning to show her the answer to her question. Despite her turmoil over Grant, she couldn't help smiling at the clever animal.

"Tell me the truth now—you're really in charge around here, right?" she said to the dog. "You just let everybody else think they're running things."

He yipped again, and waited with every evidence of impatience for her to reach the smaller barn's door. She knew he usually got in through an opening left for just that reason in the equipment room at the far end, so Mercy had to assume—with a rueful grin— that he was not certain this witless human could find her way without his help.

She slid back the heavy door, and Gambler darted inside. He halted in front of the foaling stall and waited while she closed the door behind her.

"Such a gentleman," she complimented him. "I wish your owner was a little more—"

She cut herself off. She was *not* going to do this. She was not going to blame Grant for her hurt feelings. She'd brought this on herself. He'd never made any secret about his feelings.

Her mouth twisted wryly. She'd never been one for recreational sex, but apparently she'd indulged last night, even though she hadn't realized it at the time.

Or perhaps she just hadn't wanted to realize it.

With a sigh, she walked over to the stall, wondering how the night that had seemed so perfect when she last set foot here had turned into such a mess.

Lady was on her feet, and she looked calmly at Mercy as she came up to the door. That was the hallmark of all the horses on Grant's ranch, it seemed, this calmness that spoke of gentle handling.

Her heart gave a little skip. Where was the foal? She leaned over the open bottom of the Dutch door and peered around the stall. Nothing. Then a movement on the far side of the leopard mare turned her head that way. And a second later a tiny face peered back at her from the safety of her mother's solid form.

Mercy smiled widely, relieved and utterly charmed. "Hello there, little one," she crooned. "Merry Christmas."

The little ears flicked madly at the new sound.

"You, too, Mama." She held out the piece of apple she'd brought. The mare stretched her neck out to sniff it, then delicately nibbled it off Mercy's palm.

She heard the big door slide open again. She didn't look. None of the hands were due back until late, so she knew it had to be Grant, but the mare's suddenly alert look and Gambler's immediate defection toward the door proved her guess.

He said nothing, but she heard him moving around, then heard the water go on, and a stirring sound. A few more sounds, and then footsteps.

The mare whickered softly as Grant approached.

"Sorry I'm late, Mama," he murmured as he opened the stall door. Mercy saw then that he held a large, heavy plastic tub with a thick layer of what looked like steaming oats or something in the bottom.

"Breakfast?" she asked, careful to keep her voice cheerful, and trying not to think about why he was late.

"Bran mash," he said as he set it down. "She should be back on regular feed in about a week or ten days," he said, a little absently, as he looked the mare and foal over for any sign of a problem, "but this is best for her now."

"Oh."

And just like that, she was out of things to say. How could two people who had what they had done last night possibly be acting like virtual strangers now?

They stood and watched the mare clean out the tub while the little filly watched with bright-eyed curiosity. The moment she was finished, Grant removed the tub so that neither mare nor baby could get hurt. He took it back to the sink that Mercy could now see was much more than a mere convenience, and cleaned it methodically. And silently.

He hesitated for a moment after he put it back in its place. For a moment, Mercy thought he was going to speak, but at last he left without a word. With a stifled sigh, she turned back to the stall. The sight of the foal nursing hungrily made her smile, despite her tangled emotions. There was so much of hope and peace and simplicity here that she could even set aside her confusion for the moment and enjoy the simple miracle before her.

"That family you married into is too much for me, Mom. Every day's a new adventure."

Grant shifted in the ladder-back oak kitchen chair,

his feet up on the table. He had, however, pulled off his boots before doing so; his mother's training was deep and thorough.

"It is that," Barbara Fortune agreed with a good-natured laugh. "Can you believe that Monica's son, Brandon, is really the kidnapped twin? All this time, we all assumed the missing twin was a girl, like Lindsay."

"So," Grant said wryly, "did that woman who tried to pass herself off as Lindsay's sister."

"That Ducet woman? Well, the resemblance was remarkable. Perhaps it was an honest mistake."

Grant smiled, but it was a bitter expression. He didn't mention that the fact that the woman and her companion had vanished so completely when Brandon Malone came forward with the letter from Monica made that likelihood remote at best. No, the Ducet woman had been after money. And he didn't see much difference between her approach and that of the women who took one look at the size of the M Double C and decided he'd be a nice trophy to add to their walls.

But his mother was always looking for the good in people, whether it was there to find or not.

"So Monica was behind it all?" he asked. "Even Kate's death?"

Barbara Fortune sighed, and Grant wondered if she was having trouble finding any good to ameliorate what the bitter, obsessed woman had done.

"According to the letters found in the safe-deposit box and what Gabe Devereax, the family's detective, has discovered, she was obsessed with gaining control of Kate's company. She thought it was Brandon's birthright. And she hated Kate, because Ben would never leave her.''

''So Monica paid her back by engineering the hijacking that killed her. Charming.'' He shifted in the chair uncomfortably. He didn't know how his mother lived in such a world. He didn't even like hearing about it, although he certainly welcomed the distraction this morning. ''I suppose she was behind all that trouble at the lab, too?''

''She wrote about that, as well. She was hoping the sabotage would throw things into chaos and she could take advantage of it.''

The Fortunes were always in chaos, Grant thought wryly. ''I wish Brandon Malone luck,'' he said. ''He's going to need it, to deal with that family.''

''They're my family, too, Grant.''

He let out a compressed breath. ''I know. I'm sorry.''

''And yours, as well.''

''I've never felt like they are.''

''I know. But they admire you, in their own way.''

''Me?'' Grant asked, startled.

''Nate's always said he liked your backbone. And you know Kate thought of you as family. She left you that horse, after all.''

Joker. Yes, she had. She'd left him the stallion, the horse that could turn the ranch from just a profitable operation into a gold mine. The horse who had been charmed by a petite lady cop. The same small but potent package who had turned his life upside down.

''I still don't know why she did it,'' he said, dragging his mind away from a subject he wasn't ready to deal with at the moment.

"Kate was a generous woman."

Something in his mother's voice made him speak quickly. "I'm sorry, Mom. I know you cared a great deal for her. I didn't mean to sound ungrateful. I'm just...still amazed, I guess."

"I've always been afraid that you've felt a bit...left out."

"Not like that," Grant assured her. "If anything, I'm grateful to be so far removed from all this melodrama. I'm just a simple cowboy. I can't handle all these machinations."

"Simple cowboy, my boots," his mother said, but Grant could almost see her grinning. Then he heard her sigh before she said, "I just wish Kate could have lived to see this. She would have rejoiced to know her baby was alive and well."

"Baby? Isn't he pushing forty by now?"

"Well, you know what I mean. Everyone's always referred to him that way, since he was kidnapped practically before Kate even got to hold him. Besides, when it's your child and you love him, he's always your baby."

"Yes, Mother," Grant said dutifully, but he was smiling in spite of himself, reading her obvious message. He'd never doubted his mother's love, because she took every opportunity such as this one to remind him it would never fail him. "So, was Ben really in on the kidnapping plot all along?"

"So the letter Monica left Brandon—I still can't believe he's Kate's son—says. Monica couldn't have kids, and when she heard Kate was having twins, well, she blackmailed Ben into giving her Brandon. I can't believe he hurt the family that way."

Grant grimaced. "I wouldn't mind being related to Kate, but I'm not sure I'd want to claim Ben Fortune even if I had to."

His mother was silent. For too long. Grant's feet came down to the floor. "Mom? What's wrong?"

"We've...found out something else. It was all over the news here a few months ago, but you probably never heard how come Jake was giving in to Monica's demands. It came out when Jake was arrested for Monica's murder."

Grant muttered under his breath; he'd had about enough of the Fortune family's dramatics. They were worrying his mother, and he didn't like that. Maybe he could get her to come to the ranch for a visit, to get away from all the turmoil that seemed to follow the Fortunes like vultures following a potential meal. But he held back for now; she had enough to worry about, with her brother-in-law in jail, facing a very high-profile murder trial.

"Now what?" was all he said.

"It's about Jake." She hesitated. He didn't push; he'd learned long ago that his mother would get to it in her own way. "We found out...he's not Ben's son."

Grant went still. "What?"

"Kate apparently was pregnant when she and Ben married. But it wasn't Ben's child. Jake's real father was killed in the war."

Grant let out a low whistle. "So what does that mean? Jake's not the heir to the Fortune...fortune?"

"I'm not certain. Things are...a bit confused."

"I'll bet. How's Nate taking it? He was always trying to go Jake one better, but this..."

"He's...acting very odd. He's been to see Jake, but he hasn't told me yet what they've talked about."

"Mom—"

"Oh, he will. Eventually. Your stepfather has his own way of doing things."

Your stepfather. Funny, even though his mother had been married to Nate for twenty-five years, he still couldn't quite bring himself to consider the dynamic, powerful and just a bit too hungry Nate Fortune as his stepfather.

"Jake and Erica look like they're reconciling."

Grant's jaw dropped. "What?"

"This has really drawn them back together. I think Jake realizes now that he really needs her. And they do love each other."

"I'm...amazed."

He was also glad, but he wasn't quite sure why. He'd never quite understood why Erica had put up with Jake's demanding personality as long as she had. But the news that even through the current adversity they were still fighting to make it work made him feel inexplicably cheerful.

"Things will work out," his mother said with her usual optimism. "So how is your guest doing?"

"Mercy?" As if there were somebody else, he thought wryly. But he didn't have an answer to the question, so he was stalling.

"Mercy? My, I haven't heard that since you were kids."

"I... We've kind of gotten back in the habit."

"Is she doing all right? Kristina was very worried about her."

"I think she's dealing with...that."

"That's good to hear. She's a wonderful girl—I hate to think of her hurting. Is she there? Kristina will be here in a minute, and I'm sure she'll want to talk to her."

"Er...she's outside. Wait a second." He set the receiver down and got to his feet. "Gambler," he said as he walked toward the door. The dog, who had been dozing on the small rug in front of the sink, scrambled to his feet. "Mercy," Grant said. The dog trotted across the room as Grant opened the door. "Find her, boy. Find Mercy."

Gambler gave the muffled yip that meant he understood. He watched the animal dart through the door, then lope toward the barn as if he knew exactly where she would be. No doubt he was right, Grant thought. She'd been enchanted by the new foal. Besides, Gambler always knew the whereabouts of everyone in his world. His nice, ordered world.

Grant suddenly wasn't sure the dog wasn't a lot better off than his supposed master.

Twelve

Mercy didn't know how long she'd spent standing there watching the foal, who was now fairly steady on her feet, when Gambler appeared at her side again. He yipped as if to get her attention, then trotted toward the door. He paused, looking back over his shoulder at her expectantly. Then he yipped again, took a few more steps, and repeated the pattern.

"I'm supposed to follow you, right?" Mercy said. She took a couple of steps toward the dog, and he immediately barked in approval and started off again. Mercy laughed, unable to help herself. "Lead on, dog. I've always loved Lassie movies."

It was quickly obvious that the animal was heading back to the house. For a moment, when she remembered the last time Gambler had issued a summons, her heart sped up. Was something wrong? Had Grant been hurt, or—?

She broke off her thoughts with a wry quirk of her mouth. *You've watched too* many *of those Lassie movies,* she told herself sternly. Still, she picked up her pace as she followed the mottled gray dog as he led her around to the kitchen.

"—much better, I think."

She heard his voice the instant she stepped inside and was, perhaps foolishly, relieved to see him sitting in one of the chairs at the oak table, the telephone cradled on his shoulder.

"Yes, she is," he said, glancing over at her. "Here, she can tell you herself."

He got up and held the receiver out to her. Mercy blinked, startled.

"Kristina," he said. He bent to scratch Gambler's ear. "Good boy," he said.

Mercy's eyes widened. "You really…sent him for me? And he did it?"

"He knows who you are, and he knows the command 'Find.' It's nothing special, for him."

She knew it was only her touchy mood this morning that made her read more than he'd meant into that "nothing special," as if he'd meant it to apply to her, as well, but that didn't stop the sting of it. She took the phone none too gently, ignoring Grant's startled look before he left the room to let her talk in private.

"Meri?"

It took her a moment. She'd gotten used to Mercy, and the other name sounded odd now. "Hello, Kristina. Merry Christmas."

"You, too," her friend said. "I tell you, it's been quite a time here. There's so much going on. Dad's in shock about Uncle Jake and Grandfather, Mom's trying to help him…but Grant can tell you all that. Mom just told him everything. Tell me about you. How are you doing?"

"I'm fine." It wasn't really a lie, she thought. As far as what Kristina was worried about was concerned, she was fine. It was the rest of her life that had suddenly gotten confused.

"You don't sound fine," Kristina said.

Mercy, shrugging off her heavy jacket in the warmth of the kitchen, hastened to head her off. "I am, really. I feel...much better about Nick now. I'm handling it."

"No more nightmares?"

Mercy's hand tightened around the receiver as she remembered the night the horrid dream had chased her from the house. Remembered the way Grant had gently, almost tenderly, held her, soothed her, until the ugliness faded.

"They've gone, I think," she said softly.

"Then it did help. I thought it might. You always were the type who had to go off alone and work your way through things."

Sometimes Kristina's perceptiveness surprised her, Mercy thought. It was easy to dismiss her as a spoiled, beautiful princess, but there was more to the pretty blonde than that.

"And Grant's a good listener," Kristina added.

Yes, Kristina was full of surprises. "Yes," she agreed, "He is."

"We really miss him, but I'd hate to think of you alone out there. I'm glad he stayed."

Mercy's throat was suddenly tight. "I'm sorry if I...kept him from his usual plans."

"Don't worry. It's more important that you're not alone. And it's not like Grant likes it here. He only comes every year to see us."

She'd suspected this, perhaps even known it. The clues had been clear; the men's reaction to the Christmas preparations, Rita's comments, all of it, but still, this confirmation that Grant had forgone his usual family visit for her sake, so that she wouldn't be alone, moved her almost beyond words.

"If he had his way," Kristina said, her tone one of bewildered affection, "I don't think he'd ever leave that silly ranch of his."

Mercy swallowed hard, past the lump in her throat. "I want to thank you for...suggesting I come here. It's been wonderful. Peaceful. And it's so beautiful."

"Beautiful? Peaceful I'll believe, but beautiful? Don't forget, I've been there."

"It's really quite lovely. With the snow—"

"We've got snow here, too, but at least it's covering something interesting. Not just barns and fences and cows."

"Cattle," Mercy said.

"Oh, Lord, you sound like Grant. Don't tell me you actually *like* it there? There's not a decent store in what passes for the nearest town, and not a decent manicurist for miles."

"Spoken like a true city girl," Mercy said, then wished she could call back the words.

But Kristina only laughed. "Well, I am." Then, suddenly serious, she asked, "That sounds like Grant talking again. Is he still...bitter?"

"Bitter?"

"About city girls."

"I... He doesn't seem to like them much."

"After what that Carter witch did, I'm not surprised."

Mercy held her breath. She'd known there had to be something, or someone, behind Grant's dislike; it had seemed far too specific and concentrated for there not to be.

He has his reasons.

Rita's words came back to her again. Obviously, one of those reasons was a woman named Carter.

"Carter?" Mercy asked, trying to keep her tone one of only mild interest, and hoping Kristina's natural volubility would do the rest.

"Constance Carter. She belongs to my father's country club. That's how she met Grant, a few years ago. She acted like she was really taken with him, but he was nothing but a curiosity to her, somebody she could drag to parties and show off as her latest novelty, a handsome, wealthy cowboy. But when she found out he had no intention of leaving the ranch and living in the city as her...trophy husband, she dropped him. Said she couldn't believe he'd really expected her to live in such an uncivilized place."

Kristina's voice rang with remembered outrage; most might see only the surface beauty and the easy charm, but Mercy had always known family loyalty ran strong and deep in Kristina Fortune. So strong that she didn't even see the irony in her own words, since she felt the same way about the ranch as did the despised Constance Carter.

"Well, it is pretty isolated out here," Mercy said.

"You don't have to tell me," Kristina said with a laugh. "I've been there, remember? When Grant asked me to stay one whole summer, I lasted about three weeks. I don't know how Mom lived there as long as she did. She's much happier in the city, with people around."

It hit Mercy then, hard. The three women Grant had cared for most in his life, his mother, his sister, and a woman he'd apparently loved enough to propose to, and he'd lost them all to the city. Or so it must seem to him. No wonder he was bitter, no wonder he spoke those words *city girl* like an epithet. And she found she couldn't blame him.

It wasn't until she had finished her conversation with Kristina, and said a brief hello to Kristina's mother and wished her happy holidays, that something else struck her. She hung up the phone, picked up her jacket and walked slowly back outside, thinking. Wondering.

Had Grant's reaction this morning, his words about expecting nothing more from her except that she would go back to her other life, not been meant as a warning after all? At least not for her? Had it rather been a warning aimed at him, a reminder that she, like all the women in his life, would go back to the city? Had he merely been anticipating what he saw as inevitable, and trying to make it less painful for both of them?

What he saw as inevitable?

Her own thoughts rang in her head. She walked on, pulling her jacket on and buttoning it against the brisk air.

He was right, wasn't he? It was inevitable. She would go back. She had to. Not just to face Nick's killers when they were captured, but to face her own demons, unleashed in the moments when she had realized she was too late to do anything to save him, the moments when Nick had breathed his last, rasping breath in her arms.

She shivered, violently, and it had nothing to do with the cold; the sun was bright and warm, even on this winter day, with snow all around. She sped up her steps, even though she knew that it would do little to warm this kind of chill.

Of course she would go back. Her life, her work, was there. What else would she do? Hide out here forever? A burst of unexpected longing exploded within her at the idea of staying here, forever, with Grant.

"Coward," she snapped at herself, and began to walk even faster. "You really did leave your nerve back in that warehouse, didn't you?"

Her jaw tight, her head down, she hurried until she was almost running. Finally her gasping lungs forced her to slow down, reminding her again that good shape in barely eight-hundred-feet-above-sea-level Minneappolis didn't necessarily translate to good shape in a state where the average elevation was seven thousand feet.

She hadn't consciously realized where she was heading, but when she at last noticed her surroundings, she wasn't surprised. She kept on, wishing she had Joker's long legs and power to carry her, but realizing she would never dare take the big horse out alone. And alone was what she needed to be right now.

She'd never felt so overwhelmed by so many conflicting emotions in her life. She'd been devastated by Nick's death, consumed by her own feelings of guilt over it, her own doubts about the path she'd chosen. But she'd been handling it. Perhaps not well, but she had been handling it.

It was only when she came here, only when the peaceful beauty of this place and the powerful presence of the man who owned it were added to the brew, that it had all boiled over, spilling in so many directions. She felt so scattered she didn't know if she could ever pull herself together again.

She had to take her hands out of her pockets to make the short climb up to the protected shelf that overlooked the ranch, but she shoved them back into the warmth as soon as she reached it. It was here, of all the quiet places Grant had shown her, that she had found the most peace.

Was it odd, that where others seemed to find only isolation, she found a welcome solitude? Was there something strange about her, some missing part that made her find serenity where others had found only loneliness? That while others seemed to talk out their problems unceasingly, she preferred a quiet, secluded place to think about her life...and what she was going to do with the rest of it?

I used to come up here a lot. When my dad was sick, I used to...hide out up here, when things got to be too much.

Grant's words flowed over her as if he were there, speaking them again, in that tone of quiet understanding. He knew, he felt the same way. She wasn't really alone. And perhaps she wasn't as odd as she'd feared.

But she'd been right about the scars he carried. Although he carried them so much more gracefully than she, Mercy thought with a sigh as she looked out over the landscape that was so familiar now, yet no less pleasing for that.

She drew her knees up in front of her and wrapped her arms around them, tucking her hands into her sleeves. She'd stopped to change into a warmer sweater and a pair of heavier socks—and a bra, because going without reminded her too vividly of the moment when Grant had first bared her breasts and groaned in pleasure—but she'd managed to forget her gloves in the process. But it wasn't nearly as cold here in her granite shelter as it was out where the wind was all too willing to show its opinion of people who hadn't the sense to stay inside where it was warm.

Well, if she'd had any sense, as her father was wont to say, she wouldn't have become a cop in the first place. And she wasn't sure he hadn't been right, although once she'd made it, Gordon Brady had been as proud of her as if the uniform had been his own dream for her all along.

She sighed, feeling a tug of longing for her father's wry wisdom and her mother's quiet support. But if she'd gone to them, she wouldn't have had this time with Grant. And whatever happened now, she didn't think she would ever want to give that up. Not for anything, despite the confusion she'd been hurled into now, would she give up the memory of what had come to life between them. Especially when it might be the only thing to get her through what could be some dark, grim days ahead.

She let out a long sigh. In the beginning, she'd always been glad to get back to the job after days off, and more so after a vacation. But lately, the constant contact with nothing but the negative side, nothing but the misery, had begun to wear on her, to erode her very faith in people's innate goodness, until there was very little left, until she dreaded going back to work.

Her colleagues told her that was life on the job and

she'd better get used to it, but she didn't know if it was possible to get used to the ugliness, day in and day out, if it was possible to deal with it and not have it rub off on you one way or another. You either became so hardened to it that you didn't care about anything anymore, or you let it eat at you until you hated not only your fellow human beings, but yourself, as well. Either way, you were no good to anyone after that. In fact, you were a danger. There was only one thing worse.

A cop who'd lost the nerve.

She shivered, rubbing at her arms for a moment. She wondered if maybe she should start back; she'd been out here for—

A snorting whinny interrupted her thoughts. Joker, she thought, amazed that she, who had known next to nothing about horses such a short time ago, could now pick one out simply by the sound, with perfect certainty.

And if it was Joker, then of course it was Grant. She bit her lip, and with an effort managed to keep her expression even as she waited. A moment later, man and horse appeared. Grant pulled the big Appy to a halt in the same spot he'd stood in before. When he spoke, his voice was quiet, and so neutral she knew it had to take a conscious effort.

"I thought you might be up here."

"I...needed to think."

Something flickered across his face, some emotion she couldn't pin down before it vanished.

"Mercy, if it's about this morning—"

"No. I mean...not entirely," she added honestly.

"That's part of it, but it's really—" she waved her hand rather vaguely "—everything."

Grant was silent for a moment, looking at her. "Everything?" he finally asked, his voice still quiet and soft.

She stared past him, out over the snowy ranch, and on to the horizon. Only the bases of the mountains were visible today, as clouds clung to the peaks.

"I feel like...I've found myself and lost myself at the same time," she murmured, knowing even as the words came out that they made no sense at all.

Grant said nothing. What was there to say after a silly statement like that? Mercy wondered. But then he nudged Joker, and the horse executed a neat sidling step, until Grant's knee was nearly touching the edge of the rocky shelf. Grant swung his right leg over the horse's back, and with one small movement was sitting beside her. He tossed the reins over the horse's head, and Joker's head dropped as he settled in to patiently wait.

For a while, they just sat there, each staring outward. As if they were both afraid to look at each other, Mercy thought, wondering if it was true.

Grant cleared his throat. She glanced at him in time to see him open his mouth as if to speak, then close it again. He let out a breath, then tried again.

"Coming here was supposed to...help you," he said.

"It has," she said earnestly. "It's helped so much. I can think about Nick now and...not cry. I don't have the nightmares about what happened, not anything like before. I've found peace here, Grant. A peace I never expected to find."

"If that's what you've found..." He hesitated, as if he didn't really want to ask the question, and when he went on, his tone was forced. "What have you lost?"

Mercy sighed. Grant went still. He waited for a moment, then said stiffly, "None of my business, right?"

"No, it's not that!" She drew up her knees again, and hugged them to her. "It's just that...when I think of going back, of going out there on the job again, it's not like it used to be. I knew that, even before Nick, but I kept telling myself it was only temporary, that I was going through burnout, like every cop does at one time or another."

"But you don't think that now?"

Slowly, reluctantly, she shook her head. "Since I've been here...since I've seen the peace and beauty here...I know it's more than that." She closed her eyes, resting her chin on her knees. It was hard to admit this, but she knew deep inside that if there was anyone who wouldn't judge her, it was Grant.

"I'm afraid I've...I've lost my nerve for my job."

"You? No way."

He sounded so incredulous, Mercy couldn't help feeling slightly warmed inside. But not even Grant's astonishment at the idea made it go away.

"Thank you. But I can't change how I feel. I used to be eager to go back, ready to get out there and do battle, to try and clean things up. But now, I just wonder what's the point? People will just keep on doing what they do, and my little bit won't even slow them down."

"People aren't all like that," Grant said.

"I know. But those are the ones cops see. It's the nature of the job. And the thought of dealing with more slime like the bastards who murdered Nick...it doesn't make me glad that I might play a part in putting them away, it just makes me...sick."

She felt Grant's hand on her shoulder, and then he turned her to face him.

"You haven't lost your nerve for the job, Mercy," he said softly. "You've lost your stomach for it. That's an entirely different thing."

She looked up at him, and saw in his eyes all the comfort and gentle understanding she ever could have wished for in this crisis of confidence. And she knew then that he'd only been trying to rescue them both from an uncomfortable disillusionment by confronting head-on the knowledge that there was no future for them. And that he'd been willing to risk it anyway made her feel... She wasn't sure how it made her feel. And knowing that there was no future for them didn't make it any easier to understand. Even if she was willing to leave her entire life behind, she doubted Grant would ever really trust a city girl to stay.

"You've got more nerve than anybody I know, Mercy," he said, his gaze never wavering. "Don't ever doubt that. But you're also...compassionate. You feel things, deeply. And maybe you've just simply had enough of trying to solve problems for people who don't care or don't want their problems solved."

She whispered his name, then stopped, unable to think of another thing to say. Then, slowly, not sure she should but unable to stop herself, she stretched upward and kissed him. She felt him go still, and wondered if she'd managed to make her problems worse. But then he was kissing her back, warmly, welcomingly, his arms coming around her as he hauled her against him.

At the first flick of his tongue over her lips, Mercy parted them for him. She welcomed his probing exploration, and savored the sound of satisfaction he made as she tasted him in turn, teasing the rough velvet of his tongue with the tip of her own. She felt his hands move to cup her head, then heard him grunt in frustration. He pulled back just long enough to tug off his heavy gloves; then, before she could do more than drag in a breath, he threaded his fingers through her hair. She'd left it down, more aware of the silken length of it than ever before in her life, after Grant's whispered words last night about how beautiful it looked and how good it felt trailing over his skin.

He pulled her head back and took her mouth again, fiercely this time. There was nothing tentative about this; he kissed her like a man staking a claim. And she let him, feeling for the first time in her life the wish that a man, this man, would do just that.

She clung to him, kissing him back hungrily, not caring that she was betraying every bit of her need for reassurance. Not caring about anything but this man and the way he made her feel. And when one strong hand slid down to unbutton her jacket, she didn't protest, but shifted to make it easier for him. And when he slipped his hand inside to cup her breast, she gave a tiny cry of gladness and pressed herself against his palm, wishing only that it was his hand on her naked flesh, without the interference of the layers of clothing.

Grant slipped to his side and pulled her down beside him, onto a bed of leaves and sweet-scented pine. Mercy wriggled to get closer to him, wondering how she could ever have thought this small, protected place the least bit cold. It was more than warm now; she half expected the granite overhang to be glowing with their reflected heat.

They reached for each other at the same moment, tugging at each other's shirts, freeing them from jeans that were suddenly far too confining. When seeking hands at last found bare skin, their sighs of relief were simultaneous. Mercy traced the muscled planes of his belly and chest, but stopped with a gasp when Grant found and held her breast, rubbing his thumb over her nipple until even the thin lace of her bra seemed far too much fabric.

Her hands slipped convulsively down to his waist, and held on as he continued to tease the taut peak until heat was rippling through her. Her fingers tightened, pulling him closer. He grasped her wrist with his free hand and gently moved her hand, pressing her palm over his straining erection. Mercy felt the heat of him even through the denim, and traced his length with a slow thoroughness that made him groan. She did it again, reaching tentatively lower, caressing, until his hips jerked convulsively.

"Mercy..." he gasped out.

She repeated the motion, and his hands shot to her shoulders, holding her still.

"Mercy, stop."

"You don't...like that?"

He laughed, low and harsh. "You're about to find out how much I like it, right here on this damn rock."

She took one look at the heat that was glowing in

his eyes, glanced around the sheltered alcove that magically seemed to be blocking the cold and welcoming what warmth there was from the winter sun, then looked back at his face and smiled.

"A little chilly, maybe, but...I think I like the idea."

Grant groaned again, as deeply as he had when she caressed him, as if her words had affected him as much as her touch had.

"If I thought for a minute you meant that..." he began, his voice rough.

"But I did," she said softly. "This place is...special."

She didn't say that she would treasure such a memory in the time ahead, when she left this place, and him, but she suspected he realized it anyway. Something flickered in his eyes, something in their blue depths that told her he, too, was thinking of memories as yet unmade. And, she admitted to herself, there was an utterly selfish motive driving her; she wanted some memory of her always to be with him, imprinted on this special place, the memory of at least one city girl he hadn't hated.

And then Grant was moving, so swiftly she barely had time to realize what he was doing, and so swiftly she wouldn't have time to protest, even had she wanted to. She didn't want to. He tugged off her jacket and shoved it beneath her, to cushion her from their granite bed. He paused to kiss her, deep and hot and enflaming, before he tugged at the snap of her jeans, then at the zipper, his fingers clumsy, as they never were in his haste. Mercy reached to help him, but he brushed her hands away, urging them to his own zipper.

In her eagerness, her hands were clumsy, too, but eventually she managed the button at his waist, and after that the insistent press of his flesh helped her with the zipper. She pushed aside the interfering clothing, and then she had him in her hands, hot and hard and satin-smooth. Grant let out a harsh groan as she stroked him, as her fingers curled around his length and her thumb rubbed over the swollen tip of him, spreading his own ardent moisture.

He clawed at her jeans and panties then, dragging them down her legs. Mercy knew this would be awkward, that this was insane, trying to make love on a rock in jeans and boots, but she didn't care—unless he made her wait too long. Already the ache inside her was unbearable, the ache that only he could ease, the hollowness only he could fill.

"Mercy," he gasped out. "Stop. That feels too damn good. I can't take any more."

He stopped her hands, still busily caressing his rigid flesh, with his own, and moved them safely to his chest. He grabbed at her left boot and yanked it from her foot with a single fierce motion, then freed her leg from the tangle of clothing. She shivered, not from the cold—it didn't seem cold at all—but from her body's sudden knowledge that it wasn't going to be denied, that she would soon have him inside her again, that he would fill her, stretch her to that exquisite fullness, then drive her to madness and beyond.

Grant shed his own big, heavy jacket and draped it over them both. He moved over her then, and shoved at his own clothing. When he lowered himself and Mercy felt the first touch of eager male flesh, she gave a glad cry and lifted herself to him. Grant covered her mouth with his, drinking in that cry, and she felt him shudder as he slid into her welcoming heat.

It truly was insane, Mercy thought in some vague part of her mind that wasn't already consumed with the driving power of Grant's body as he thrust into her again and again. Somehow the insanity of it added a new dimension, as if the setting, this high rocky shelf, for all its sheltering still in the middle of all the wild beauty around them, added a kind of wildness to their mating that could only be found in a place like this. They became as their surroundings, primal, fierce, clawing at each other as they each took and demanded and gave and gloried in all of it.

And in the end, as they exploded together, Grant's harsh shout of her name, and her keening moan of his, melded into a single primitive cry as wild as anything that lived in this untamed place.

Maybe he could stand it, Grant thought as Mercy clung to him as they rode Joker back to the ranch. Maybe he could stand the city in small doses, stand to be away from the ranch. Maybe he could take it enough to keep some kind of relationship going. Mercy seemed to truly like it here, and although he knew better than to think she'd adapt completely and want to stay forever, maybe she'd visit often enough that they could force some kind of a future out of what had flared between them.

He didn't think she'd ever force him to a choice, as Constance had. She was too open and honest for that, and he knew she realized his heart was here and always would be.

But what would be the point? A long-distance relationship composed mostly of airplane flights and phone calls, periods of aching longing broken up by bouts of fierce togetherness, where the passion of absence blurred the reality of day-to-day living together, that process by which two people really joined to form a third entity that was stronger than the sum of its parts?

His mother had that, however unlikely it seemed, with Nate. He'd had to admit that whenever he saw the driven, hungry man turn to putty in his mother's loving hands. Nate had rather belligerently told him once, during one of his Christmas visits as an equally belligerent teenager, that Barbara was his touchstone with real life, and that Grant had better get used to the idea. That had probably been the first time he truly accepted the fact that his mother was indeed a Fortune, in more than just name only. And that the powerful and sometimes star-crossed family was part of his life, like it or not.

It hit him then: Could the unexpectedly successful match of his down-to-earth, warm, sincere mother with the hungry, edgy, discontented Nate Fortune be any more unlikely than him and Mercy? Were the cowboy and the cop any more implausible a couple? Could they make something of this, as his mother and Nate had? As even Jake and Erica had, strife-torn though their lives were?

All the old warnings rose up inside him, but couldn't seem to make their way through the lingering heat that still warmed him after their passionate love-making in that spot that had always been, as Mercy had said, special. And now, he thought, it would be forever linked with Mercy in his mind, linked with her sweet, honest giving and the incredible, astonishing pleasure he'd found with her, a pleasure unlike anything he'd ever known.

He might be a fool to think anything could ever come of this, but maybe he'd be an even bigger fool to turn his back on it. Even if it didn't, couldn't, last, even if it was only for whatever time she was here.

Joker let out a whicker as they came in sight of the barn. Mercy still said nothing, and Grant wondered what she was thinking. Was she regretting what they'd done, those moments of fiery madness when they'd taken each other like two creatures born more of the wild places than the supposedly civilized people they were?

"Mercy?"

"What?" She sounded...odd, but not upset.

"I think we need to talk."

"Yes."

"I'll be in as soon as I put up Joker."

"All right," she said, still with that odd note in her voice that he couldn't label.

He dropped her off at the house and went to rub down and stable Joker, giving the stallion a scoop of sweet feed as a reward for his patience while two humans ignored him in their self-absorption. He checked on the mare and foal, pleased to see that the wary baby, who was marked so much like her father, was not at all bothered by his presence.

When he walked back into the house, he found Mercy in the den. And when he coupled the phone in her hand with the look on her face, he wished he'd never had that phone line run in that five miles from the main road.

She glanced up as he came in, but said nothing, clearly listening intently. At last she said, "Yes, I'll let you know exactly when," and hung up.

She turned to face him. He knew what was coming, and guessed she knew he knew, but she said it anyway. As if it wouldn't be real until she did.

"They've caught the murderers. The preliminary hearing is set for Monday. I have to go back."

Thirteen

If he kept on like this, Grant thought, the whole damn place was going to fall down around his ears. This had to stop. He had to keep his mind on his work, not spend half his day staring into space, thinking about Mercy, wondering if she was all right. And wondering what would have happened if they'd had the chance to have that talk.

A chill seized him, making him shiver with its ferocity. Why hadn't she told him? How could she just walk back into that deadly mess, knowing how much danger she was in?

He lugged his saddle inside and slammed the tack room door shut, making Walt, who was sitting mending a bridle strap—the kind of chore Mercy had taken off their hands—jump.

"You'd best get rid of what's eatin' you, boy," the old hand said, "while there's still something left."

"Nothing's eating me."

"Right. That's why you been snarly as a caged bobcat ever since that little lady left."

Grant dumped his saddle unceremoniously on its rack. "I'm not snarly."

Walt studied him for a moment, then said quietly, "We're all worried about her, Grant. Ever since that detective fella told you what was really going on."

Grant swore, low and harsh, his voice echoing with frustration. He'd only called Gabe Devereax, the private investigator Rebecca Fortune had hired to look into Kate's death, because his mother had said the man had friends on the police force, and Grant had wanted to make sure Mercy had people looking out for her during the preliminary hearing for the suspected killers.

It was then that he'd found out that the murder of Nick Corelli, and the previous murder of his friend, had been mob-related. Found out that Mercy herself was now, as the only witness, a target. Found out that attempts had already been made to silence her permanently, and that this, as much as her need for a place to recoup, had been behind her retreat to the M Double C; her superiors had ordered her out of town and out of sight, for her own safety.

He swore again as he yanked open a drawer beneath the small workbench and dug out a small tin of saddle soap. He'd clean the damn thing from stirrup to horn; that ought to keep him occupied.

"You gonna keep slamming around here swearin' a blue streak, or do what you want to do?"

Grant glared at the old man. "And just what might that be?"

Walt refused to be intimidated. "Go after her."

That that was exactly the urge he'd been fighting ever since Mercy had packed her bag and decamped the day after Christmas didn't make him any less testy about it. He'd decided against it more times than he could count already, yet the idea kept returning, as determined and hardheaded as the lady herself.

"She's the cop, not me. She's trained to handle—"

Walt interrupted him sharply. "Mobsters?"

Grant suppressed another shiver. Just the thought made him queasy—Mercy, facing some shadowy gangster type alone...

"You know her," he muttered. "Do you really think she'd appreciate me charging after her like she was a child who couldn't take care of herself?"

"Just because you *can* take care of yourself don't mean you always want to do it alone."

For a long, silent moment, Grant just stood there looking at the old hand. Walt met his gaze steadily, and then something oddly soft came into his eyes.

"I'd hate to see you end up like your daddy, son. He lost once and never tried again, just got old and died here, all alone except for you and me. But you and I both know there was a big part of him that died a long time ago, when your mamma left."

"Damn." Grant swore a third time, but this time it was in a tone of surrender.

Walt smiled. "You go to it, boy. We'll keep things runnin' around here. You ain't been much help of late, anyway."

Four hours later, he was fastening his seat belt on a small turboprop plane headed for Denver and his connecting flight to Minneapolis. And he wasn't sure if he was happy about it or not. He only knew he couldn't do anything else.

Mercy had given up trying to read the book that lay open on her lap; in any case, the light in her bedroom had faded long ago. Nor was there any point in going over the paperwork she'd brought home from her meeting with the detectives and the prosecuting attorneys; she couldn't know it any better than she did now.

So she was spending her Sunday evening here in the dark, wishing she was alone instead of cooped up in her apartment with her bodyguard, who was watching the Timberwolves game in her small study until his relief arrived in a few minutes.

They'd wanted to put her in a hotel, but she'd refused. To the best of their knowledge, the men behind the men who had killed Nick didn't know where she lived, and she'd been gone long enough to throw them off. Over her protests, however, they had insisted on a twenty-four-hour guard. Eric Neilsen was the young officer who was assigned tonight to keep her alive long enough to officially identify Nick's killers in the courtroom tomorrow morning. The young officer who was so gung ho and enthusiastic he made her feel old, despite the fact that she probably only had two or three years on him. The young officer who was so fired up even about this boring detail that it made her all the more aware of the fire she herself had lost.

The continuous patter of the basketball announcer emanating from the study was abruptly shut off in midsentence. She came instantly alert, wondering what had made the rabid fan turn off the game he'd been glued to. Then she heard what he had no doubt heard before, a rather forceful knock on the door. She closed her book and scrambled to her feet. She swept her off-duty weapon, a dark gray, lightweight seventeen-round Glock semiautomatic pistol, up off the nightstand.

"Eric?" she called.

"I'm checking."

She made her way to the door into the living room, listening intently. She heard Eric call out to whoever was there, but from her position could only hear a muffled answer through the door. She went into the living room and saw the young cop peering through the peephole, his own .45 automatic in his hand.

"I said she's not here," Eric called out. She still wasn't close enough to hear what whoever it was said, but when Eric lifted his weapon, her heart took a little leap.

"Mister, you try taking this door down, and I guarantee you'll be one sorry bastard."

Adrenaline shot through her. She ran across the room and took up a position beside the door, where she would be behind it if indeed the man was foolish enough to try to force his way in.

"This doesn't sound right," she whispered to Eric. "If they wanted in, they wouldn't be so blatant about it. Maybe I'd better check the back windows, see if this is a diversion."

"Good idea," Eric agreed. "Lousy diversion, though. That cowboy getup he's wearing stands out like crazy."

Mercy stopped in midstride. "Cowboy?"

"Dumb hat and all," Eric said. "And you'd think they'd get your name right." He gave her a rather crooked smile. "Or maybe it's just some confused drunk at the wrong apartment. Any of your neighbors named Mercy and hooked up with some clown in a cowboy hat and boots?"

She nearly dropped the Glock. "What?"

"That's what he said. That he was here to see Mercy and he wasn't leaving until he did."

"My God," she whispered, and ran back to peer through the peephole. Although she'd already guessed, his name still escaped her on a long breath. "Grant."

She shoved the weapon in the waistband of her jeans, and before Eric could even react, she had the locks off and was pulling the door open. Grant stood there, looking a bit startled at the speed with which the door finally swung open. She couldn't seem to speak, only stare at him. He took a step toward her, his arms coming up, and her pulse raced in anticipation of his embrace. But then he stopped, his eyes narrowing as he saw the Glock, and realized Eric was a bare two steps away, his weapon still in his hand.

"You know this guy?" Eric asked, looking Grant up and down doubtfully. She understood why; in his battered Stetson, heavy sheepskin jacket, jeans, and worn cowboy boots Grant hardly looked like a native of the Twin Cities.

"Yes," she said softly. "I do. Come in, Grant."

Grant eyed Eric warily, his gaze lingering pointedly on the chrome .45. The young cop hastily shoved it into his shoulder holster, and backed away from the door. Grant stepped inside, and Mercy closed the door behind him.

"It's really true, then," he said without preamble, looking from the nattily dressed but obviously well-armed Eric to the weapon tucked in Mercy's waistband. "Damn it, Mercy, why didn't you tell me?"

"Grant—"

"All that time, on top of everything else, you never bothered to mention these guys had tried to kill you. Twice."

She didn't know how he'd found out, and it didn't really matter now. "There was no reason to."

He went very still. "No reason?"

"We made sure they couldn't trace me to the ranch. No one there was ever in any danger—"

"Is that what you think this is about?" he yelped incredulously. "You've got mob hit men after you—" he gestured toward Eric "—you've got to be guarded, and you think I'm worried about that?"

"I—"

"Damn it, Mercy, don't you think I deserved to know the truth, especially after—"

He broke off suddenly, his eyes flicking sideways to Eric. The young man apparently was a bit slower than she'd thought, or perhaps just naive, because it wasn't until Mercy also turned to look at him that he caught on.

"Oh. Er, I guess I'll go finish watching the game."

He escaped to the study, but dutifully left the door partly open.

Mercy turned back to Grant. God, she'd missed him. She wanted to hug him, wanted him to hold her, just for a moment, but she knew she didn't dare. Because if she did, she'd never be able to let him go. And he had to go.

"Why did you come?" she asked abruptly.

"Why? I find out the mob's trying to kill you, and you have to ask?"

Something expanded inside her, some kernel of warmth that she'd hopelessly clung to even as she left him, telling herself she'd probably never see him again. He did care. But she'd known that; it wasn't in Grant to indulge in a casual affair, without caring for the woman. It wasn't that that made their relationship impossible, it was distance, more kinds than one.

And the fact that since she'd been back here, she'd had to confront what she'd done. Or rather hadn't done. And it wasn't so easy to forgive herself, here in the world where it had happened.

Her mind shied away from the painful subject.

"That's exactly why you have to go."

"Protecting me, Mercy? Is that what you were doing at the ranch, too, not telling me what was going on?"

She lowered her eyes. "You didn't need to know."

"Didn't need to know that besides Nick's death, you were dealing with the fact that you'd twice almost been murdered? Didn't need to know that's what you were walking back into now?"

"What could you have done?"

"Locked you up on the ranch, maybe," he said, his voice grim.

"Grant, I had to come back."

"Yeah." He shoved back the brim of his hat. "And you did it in a big hurry, too. Were you that eager to get back and become a target again? Was even that better than staying away from your precious city one more day?"

His voice was laced with an anger she didn't understand. "You know that's not true—"

"Do I?"

"You should," she countered. "I have to do this, Grant. Can't you see that? I can't change...what I didn't do, but I can help put them away."

"Mercy, stop it. I thought we'd settled this. If you'd done anything, you'd be dead, too."

"I..." She swallowed and tried again. "That was easy to say then. It was the ranch, the peace there, that made me believe. But here, where Nick lived, and seeing those reports again, seeing it written there..."

His hands came up, as if he were going to reach for her. A sharp rap on the door made them both jump. Grateful for the interruption, Mercy looked through the peephole.

"It's Eric's relief," she said, and the young cop appeared in the doorway as she reached for the dead bolt.

"Murphy?" he asked.

She nodded, and opened the door to a redheaded older man who had been one of Mercy's training officers when she first come out of the academy.

"Hi, Murph," she said.

The older man nodded to her as he stepped inside, but his attention was fixed on Grant. "Who's the cowboy?"

His tone was amused. For an instant, Mercy saw Grant as he must appear to those used to the sophisticated polish of city men. But where they saw someone to chuckle at, she saw only Grant's solid, rugged beauty, and the aura of the open, wild places she'd come to love.

Just as she'd come to love the man who now stood here, representing all she'd found in his world.

She admitted it, that she loved him, here and now in this most impossible of places and time, with a stabbing jab of pain. For Grant was also the man who deserved better than a woman who'd let a man she cared for be killed, practically before her eyes, without lifting a finger.

"He's...a friend," she said to Murphy.

The redhead turned to face her. "Get him out of here, girl."

"I'm trying."

"Stubborn, is he?"

"He also," Grant said mildly, "doesn't care much for being talked about in the third person when he's standing right here."

Murphy's brows rose, and he looked back at Grant. "Smart one, huh? It's for your own good."

"He also doesn't like being patronized."

"Mighty big words for a cowboy."

"And you've got a mighty big mouth, for a cop."

"Will you two stop?" Mercy said, exasperation overtaking her. "Murphy, knock it off. Grant's done nothing but help. He owns the ranch I went to, all right?"

"I'm out of here," Eric put in, looking at the other two men warily as he dodged past them out the door and pulled it shut behind him.

Murphy grinned suddenly. "So the cowboy bit's for real, huh? Sorry. Thought maybe you were one of those wannabe types." He glanced at Mercy. "And we're a little wound up about tomorrow."

Grant grimaced. "Maybe you should put some of that energy to work figuring out a way to put these guys away without her having to be a target."

Murphy shook his head. "No way. We're going to need her testimony. But she'll be okay. We've had that courthouse staked out and covered since the moment we caught those bastards.''

Grant didn't look particularly reassured, and somehow that warmed Mercy even more.

Murphy turned to her. ''We're going to go over it again tonight, Brady. You know they're going to try and cash in on the fact that you didn't see the actual shooting.''

''So she has to appear in public and let them have another try at her?'' Grant said, sounding more than a little belligerent.

''She'll have a squad of our special tactics team with her every step of the way,'' Murphy explained, beginning to sound a tiny bit harassed.

Then, as if something had just registered with him, Murphy seemed to suddenly shift gears, looking from Grant to Mercy and back again. A speculative look came into his eyes, and Mercy could just feel him getting ready to ask a question she didn't want to answer.

''I'll be fine,'' she said quickly, looking at Grant. ''I have to do this. Don't you see, Grant? I have to do at least this much to put them away.''

For a long, silent moment, he stood there, looking down at her. She held his gaze, pleading with him to understand.

''I can't tell you how much it means that...you came here. But you can't help me with this, Grant. No one can. I have to face it. All of it.''

Something flickered in his gaze, something that reminded her so sweetly of the quiet places he'd shown her. Something that gave her hope, although she didn't dare name what she was hoping for. Finally, with a slow, gentle movement, he lifted one hand and touched her cheek.

"You haven't lost your nerve, Mercy," he said, repeating the words he'd said that day on the ranch, in the quiet moments before passion flared between them there in that special, private place she would hold in her heart forever. She felt color rise in her cheeks at the vivid memories, and saw by the heat glowing in his gaze that he was remembering, exactly as she was.

"I have to do this," she said again, almost desperately, because all she wanted to do was go home with him. And it didn't even rattle her that she'd thought of the ranch as her home as much as his. "I have to do it. Not just for Nick. For myself."

Again he was silent for a long moment. Murphy was uncharacteristically quiet, a blessing Mercy wasn't about to question.

"All right," Grant said at last. "I think I understand. Everybody has to fight their own demons. And you'll win, Mercy. You're too strong not to."

She let out a long breath, only now aware that she'd been holding it.

"Just do something for me, will you?" he asked softly. She nodded, unable to speak. "Don't ever lose faith in yourself, Mercy. You're still a diamond. You always will be."

He said it with such quiet, unshakable certainty it shook Mercy to the core. Here, in this time and place where she'd doubted she would ever trust herself or her own courage again, he had handed them back to her, polished and shining like the gemstone he called her. There were few people in the world she trusted as she instinctively had always trusted Grant, she thought. Didn't that mean she should trust his judgment, as well?

He looked as if he were about to say something else, but then stopped himself. He turned away from her, with a sharp, short motion, and Mercy wondered if it was truly as hard for him as it looked; selfishly, she hoped it was.

Long after he left, she was still wrestling with it. Wondering if she hadn't just made a horrible mistake by sending him away. Wondering if she would ever see him again, and if he would even speak to her if she did. Wishing she could talk to someone about it.

And at last crying, because the only people she would have trusted enough to talk to about it were Nick...and Grant himself.

He'd done tougher things, Grant told himself. He just couldn't remember right now anything harder than walking away and leaving Mercy to deal with her demons in her own way. Especially when what he wanted to do had been something primitive, like throwing her over his shoulder and carrying her back to the safety of the ranch.

He'd stayed until Monday night, watching the news of the hearing from the hotel room he'd stayed in. But once he saw the cadre of officers protecting Mercy, he'd known she truly was as safe as she could be, under the circumstances. And he'd been more than shaken by her appearance; there had been little of the woman he'd come to know on the ranch in the polished, sophisticated-looking woman in the dark suit and heels and the severe, tidy pulled-back hairstyle. City girl. Pure city girl.

So he'd gone home, feeling guilty enough already at having been in the city and not gone to see his mother or Kristina. But he told himself he couldn't have faced either of them, not until he got his tangled emotions sorted out.

But he'd known, even then, when he was standing in Mercy's apartment, that only one of those emotions really mattered. The one he'd never expressed, the one he'd walked away carrying silently inside him. He wasn't sure when it had happened, maybe when she'd first climbed out of the truck and he'd seen the woman she'd become, maybe when she'd first looked out at the ranch and found beauty there...or maybe, just maybe, twelve years ago, when she looked at him as if he'd hung the moon. He supposed it didn't matter when it had happened, only that it had. And because it had, because he'd finally had to admit to himself that he loved her, he couldn't admit it to her. Not now, not when she had her own battle to fight. It would be too much, just more pressure on her when she could least afford it.

And besides, he knew, deep down inside, how she would choose, anyway. Once she'd dealt with those demons, once she'd faced them with the courage he knew was still there, that she'd only lost sight of, she would once more be the dedicated cop she'd once been. The dedicated cop who would never dream of leaving her job, or the city that was her real home.

And he would never see her again. He would lose yet another woman to the city life he could never live.

You never had her to lose, he told himself sharply

as he leaned into the brush he was running along Joker's back, making the horse turn his head back and look at him curiously. The stallion had been acting oddly ever since Mercy had left, not moping, but waiting at the far end of the corral every day, and staring at the house, as if he expected the girl with the apple-scented hair to appear at any moment.

"Don't hold your breath," Grant muttered to the big Appy. *And take your own good advice, McClure,* he added silently to himself.

And he turned his mind to the chores ahead of him, determined to keep his thoughts away from a petite, green-eyed pixie who had somehow invaded his entire life. And his heart.

Fourteen

"He should have known better."

"Yeah, but he'd been a little crazy about Franco ever since Parness bought it, a couple of years ago. Wanted to take the whole mob down by himself."

Mercy paused in the doorway, then backed up, out of sight of the three officers who were in the prosecuting attorney's office. She'd retreated to the small adjacent conference room until the adrenaline coursing through her ebbed; keeping her cool under such fierce questioning had been one of the biggest battles of her life, and she had no idea how she'd done.

"Going in there without backup, that was crazy, all right, God rest him."

"We got 'em, though. They'll be up for the max now. That judge didn't buy a word of their crap about it being an accident. And Brady—she put them away. Never let that jerk of a defense lawyer rattle her once."

"Nick always said she was a cool head."

"Maybe if he'd been more of one, he'd still be alive."

Biting her lip, Mercy moved hastily back into the office and shut the door she'd quietly opened. The utter lack of condemnation, the casual approbation of the men who had watched the preliminary, moved her beyond words. And she had to admit that hearing Nick's actions laid out in cold, merciless detail, step by step, made them sound beyond reckless to the point of being foolhardy.

She sat there in the empty conference room for a long time, wondering why she hadn't been able to see it before, why she had simply accepted the guilt her grieving mind had foisted on her. Had she just been too close to it to think clearly? Too dazed and emotionally traumatized to think it through before?

Or had it taken the quiet peace Grant's world gave her for her to see the truth?

She knew that wasn't the answer, not really. She knew that the real reason was Grant himself, that the solid strength of him, his unwavering faith in her, was what had brought her to this, this healing realization that he'd been right, that had she acted, the only thing she would have accomplished was her own death.

Perhaps she'd had to step outside herself to realize it. And she'd done that, when she fell in love all over again with Grant McClure.

A sound at the door made her rise to her feet; it seemed that it would soon be over, but perhaps the judge had called for a break. When the door swung open, Mercy wanted to sink back into her chair; she'd been expecting the attorney, or perhaps one of the officers. Certainly not Nick's widow.

Allison came toward her swiftly, and before Mercy knew what to expect had engulfed her in a fierce hug.

"Thank you," she said fervently. "They're going to pay for what they did, and it's mainly thanks to you."

"I…" She swallowed and tried again. "It's not enough. It should never have happened."

"I know that." Allison smiled sadly. "But I also know Nick was never…quite rational about those awful people after Charlie Parness was killed. He was obsessed. He got calls and went out in the middle of the night. He took chances, crazy chances…but you know that."

She had known, but she'd just seen it as another sign of Nick's dedication to his work. She'd even reassured Allison on occasion, when she expressed her worry.

"I'm sorry, Allison," Mercy said now, meaning it more than ever. "So very sorry. I should have listened to you, back then. Maybe I could have—"

Allison interrupted her sharply. "Meredith Cecelia Brady, you aren't still thinking this was somehow your fault?"

Mercy drew back, startled. "I…"

"Kristina told me she sent you off to get over that silly idea. Haven't you?"

Kristina had known this, too? Sometimes, Mercy thought, her charmingly spoiled friend was just too full of surprises.

"I loved Nick, loved him dearly, but he brought this on himself," Allison said, with the unwavering common sense that had first drawn Mercy to her. "I'd been afraid of something just like this for months. Ever since Charlie was murdered, it was like I knew he was…on borrowed time."

Mercy shivered. "I just felt so helpless. And useless."

"You listen to me, girlfriend," Allison went on

sternly. "No one knew Nick better than I did, and I know he had a world of respect for you, as an officer, as well as a friend. It would hurt him horribly to know you were tearing yourself up over this out of some mistaken idea you could have done something to stop it. And it hurts me, too, Meri. Please, don't. Don't blame yourself. No one else does. Least of all me."

Mercy felt something let go inside her, a tightness that she'd carried for so long she almost got used to it. She *had* faced her demons, and four of them would pay the penalty they deserved, because of her. Even the judge had given her an approving look after the steady, unshakable statement she gave. Her old confidence came rushing back to fill the void that ugly knot had left. And with it came the knowledge that she could go back to her old life, to her job, with all the faith in herself and her abilities that she'd once thought lost forever.

She stared at the friend whose quiet strength astounded her.

"Allison, are you all right? Really?"

"I'm getting there. Matt and Lisa help. You can't fall apart when you've got them depending on you."

"Are they…?"

"What they are, is missing their godmother. So when are you coming to see them?"

"They…want to see me?"

"Of course they do. They've lost their father. They need the rest of us to hold together for them. And they're worried about you, because they haven't seen you. They need to see that you're all right." Allison eyed her assessingly. "You are *all* right, aren't you?"

Mercy took in a deep breath. "Yes," she said softly. "Yes, I think I am."

"Good. Then you can spend New Year's with us."

"I...don't think so. I'll come by to see the kids, but then...I have something else I have to do. Something very important."

The moment the words came out, she knew even that was an understatement; nothing in her life could be more important than what she had to do.

Yes, she could go back to the life that had been so brutally interrupted. She could go back to her work with full confidence. But she couldn't go back with full dedication. Nor with her whole heart and soul. She'd left too much of both, too much of herself, back on a ranch in Wyoming.

Grant slung a bale of hay onto the flatbed truck, resigned to starting the long haul of winter feeding. If he was prone to such excesses, he'd hire a helicopter to come in and drop the darn stuff, and have it done in a couple of hours, instead of putting in two days of miserable driving through heavy snow and pure manual labor, only to turn around and start it all over again.

He heard Gambler's welcoming bark split the silence; Walt must be back from taking the leopard mare and her baby out for her first short exercise period outside the big corral. He'd watched them go, smiling at the little filly's delicate steps through snow until they reached the roadway, which was fairly free of drifts. And he'd realized as he did it that it had been a long time since he had smiled.

Shoving that realization out of his mind, he wrestled with the next bale, questioning the wisdom of having insisted on doing what would normally be a two-man job by himself. But then, he'd taken to doing a lot of things alone of late, and the hands had learned not to question him about it. Even the irrepressible Chipper and the redoubtable Walt had steered clear of him after he ungraciously snarled at them a few times. He wasn't happy with his own behavior, but he couldn't seem to control it, which made him even angrier.

He heard Joker's trumpeting whinny from the barn. The sound startled him; the horse had been nearly as snarly as he'd been feeling of late, and that particular lighthearted sound had been long unheard around here. He leaned forward to peer toward the barn, then the house, but saw nothing, and went back to work.

"Happy New Year," he muttered to no one in particular, and shoved the next bale onto the slowly growing stack. Then the next, and the next, his mood turning uglier by the minute.

He swore under his breath when realized he'd put a little too much of his angry energy into slinging the last bale; it was headed off the other side of the truck, to hit the floor and have to be picked up all over again, if it didn't fall apart and scatter hay everywhere, which he would then have to clean up. He grabbed for it, even knowing it was futile.

The bale stopped before he even touched it. And came back the other way, landing neatly atop the stack.

"Thanks," he muttered to Walt, who had to have come in just in time to save the wayward bale.

"You're welcome."

He froze in the act of pulling off his gloves. God, he was really losing it, thinking he was hearing Mercy's voice, when he knew—

She stepped out from behind the shelter of the stack of hay. He stared at her as she walked around the truck toward him. Her expression revealed nothing to him, and he wondered why she'd come. And how— he hadn't heard a vehicle, although she looked as if she could have hiked down from the main road, where the bus went by. Unlike the polished city girl he'd seen on television, she was in jeans and boots and sheepskin jacket and a dark green flannel shirt that turned her eyes the same rich shade. Only the ponytail was missing; her pale blond hair was down and free, and his body tightened instantly at the sight, remembering too clearly the silken brush of it over every intimate part of him. He fought it, and the strain made his voice harsh.

"I heard about the hearing," he said abruptly. "And the indictment. Congratulations."

She stopped a bare two feet away from him, shrugging, as if the thing that had so occupied her now meant nothing. "There's a chance they may plead out and there won't be a trial. They know the mob doesn't want the attention, and that if push comes to shove, they're expendable."

"So you did what you had to do."

"Yes. Just like you said I would."

"You were the only one who thought you couldn't." He finished yanking off his gloves. "Are you…all right?"

"Yes." He looked up at the quiet steadiness of her voice. "You were right. There really was nothing I could have done. Even Allison knew that. But I...had to get there by myself.''

"Sometimes you have to," he conceded. "So when do you go back to work?"

"Right away, I hope."

Something quietly died inside him, a last hope he hadn't even known he was harboring. He looked away from her as he shoved the gloves into his back pocket, not at all sure of his ability to keep his expression even.

"At least," she added softly, "if the boss of the M Double C is hiring."

His head snapped back around. "What?"

She gestured at the stack of hay bales. "It does look like you could use some help."

He knew he was gaping at her, but he couldn't help it. He saw her take in a long, deep breath, and she put a hand on the bed of the truck, as if she needed the support.

"There could be a problem, though," she went on, the slightest of tremors in her voice. "I'm looking for a permanent job."

Grant swallowed tightly, sure he had to be misunderstanding her. "You...already have one. Don't you?"

"I did. A job I loved, for a while. But I finally realized it was taking away more than it was giving. Taking away more than I could afford. So I quit."

He blinked. "You quit?"

She nodded. "Foolish of me, I suppose. But you know how city girls are. Crazy. But once I...faced my doubts, once I knew that I *could* go back, I didn't have to. And I realized I didn't want to. Whether I had...someplace else to go or not.''

He didn't miss the undertone in her voice when she said "city girls," just as he so often had. But he was so startled, he said only, "You really quit?"

"Yesterday."

Yesterday. She'd quit yesterday? And then come straight here?

"Mercy," he said, then stopped, still afraid he was somehow misinterpreting her.

She picked at a splinter on the wooden bed of the truck. And picked at it again, staring at it now, as if it were utterly fascinating. And Grant realized suddenly that she was as nervous as he was. Then her chin came up, and he was looking at the sassy, courageous Mercy he'd always known. And perhaps always loved.

"Did you really name the filly No Mercy?"

He blinked; she'd obviously run into Walt. "I... Yes.''

"Is that...what you want?"

Grant swallowed tightly. He owed her this. She'd come here, clearly uncertain of her reception, and that alone had taken so much nerve it made him ache a little inside.

"The name," he said, "wasn't a wish. It was more of a...lament."

Her breath caught audibly. Her green eyes widened, and the hope he saw flaring there told him what he needed to know. And suddenly he knew even more, knew that Mercy had something Constance hadn't had, something even his mother hadn't had, a fierce, determined independence. An independence that assured that if she stayed, it would be because she wanted to.

"If you really want that job, it's...open. If you're sure you know what you're getting into."

"I'm sure," she whispered. "Oh, I'm sure. If you are."

Joy leaped in him, but in this last instant he was almost afraid to reach out for it. "You handle Joker pretty well," he said, "and you did a good job when the filly was born."

"I hope there are a dozen more little ones," Mercy said, sounding a bit reckless. "This place needs them."

Grant heard his own breath catch. "Just what kind of little ones did you have in mind?"

She met his gaze steadily. "I love you," she said simply. "What kind do you think?"

Grant's eyes closed for an instant. "I...love you, too."

"I know," she said easily. His eyes snapped open. She smiled lovingly at him, the kind of smile he'd been afraid to believe in for far too long. "I figured that out when you came charging into the city, even though you hate it, just to be sure I was all right."

Grant's mouth curved into a rueful smile. "Gave myself away, huh?"

"I just didn't know if you...loved me enough to forgive me."

"Forgive you?"

"For being a city girl."

"You're not," he said solemnly, "a city girl anymore."

"And our children won't be city kids, either."

Grant couldn't stop the grin that spread over his face at the thought of a couple of rambunctious youngsters with Mercy's dauntless spirit running amok around the place.

"I'm beginning to think," he said, still grinning, "that a filly by Fortune's Fire deserves a more appropriate name."

"What did you have in mind?"

He reached for her then, at last, the fire that leaped in him at the feel of her tempered by a new tenderness he'd never dared let himself feel before. "Mercy's Fire," he suggested.

Before she could answer, he kissed her, and showed her exactly what he meant.

Epilogue

"That's the kind of blood this family needs," Sterling Foster said approvingly as he walked into the room, his slight drawl doing nothing to detract from the decisiveness of his words.

"Whatever do you mean?" Kate Fortune rose gracefully out of her chair as the tall lawyer with his thick shock of white hair, the man who had stood by her through all the ups and downs of the past couple of years, spoke.

"That McClure boy."

Kate smiled. She wasn't about to dispute Sterling's assessment, even though she often disagreed with him just for the sake of the entertaining argument. But in this case, she utterly agreed. She'd met Barbara's son only a few times, but she'd heard much about him from the daughter-in-law she'd come to love like her own blood.

And she'd heard a great deal more from her beloved granddaughter; Kristina had never been able to say enough about her wonderful big brother, and the fact that she never categorized the relationship as anything else, never called him her half brother, told Kate a great deal about how Grant regarded her in turn. And that would have been enough for Kate, even if she hadn't liked and admired him for himself. And

Sterling had agreed with her, after he met Grant, when he informed him that Kate had left him the Appaloosa stallion in her will.

"He didn't let me intimidate him," was all he'd said, but Kate knew that for Sterling that said a great deal.

"What's he done now?" she asked.

He gestured with a rolled-up copy of what Kate recognized as a stock sale catalog. "Sold that first get of Fortune's Fire for more money than any horse is worth."

Kate smiled; horses were not Sterling's cup of tea. "You think any amount is more than any horse is worth."

"True enough. But I appreciate a good business-man when I see one. He's done well with that gift of yours."

"More than you know," Kate said, still smiling. Some amazing things had happened, and her gifts to her family had accrued some results she'd never dared to hope for.

"At this rate, by the time he's got a few more of those to sell, that ranch of his will be on the map."

Kate's smile turned rather mysterious. "I think there will be at least one he'll be hanging on to. A little filly named Mercy's Fire."

"Mercy's Fire? How do you horse people come up with those names?"

"Mercy," Kate said composedly, "is Grant's nick-name for his wife."

Sterling blinked. Kate laughed; she wasn't often able to surprise him, and she enjoyed it immensely when she could.

"He went and got married? I thought Kristina swore he never would, after that Carter woman. Who did he marry? Wait—" Kate's smile widened as Sterling's quick mind made the jump "—that friend of Kristina's who went out to Wyoming? The one who helped put that slime in jail a while back?"

"Meri Brady," Kate confirmed. "Although I think Mercy is going to be her name from now on. She's a wonderful girl. Brave, gutsy, bright."

"I always liked her," Sterling conceded. "She was a good influence on Kristina."

"Who made a lovely maid of honor," Kate said, fighting a tug of emotion. Would her beloved granddaughter someday take her own trip down an aisle? Perhaps, if she went to deal with her own inheritance, if she went to California and got away from all the chaos that was happening here... Stranger things had happened, and more than once in the time since her supposed demise, her legacies to her loved ones had somehow served as the turning point in their lives.

Sterling frowned suddenly. "And just how did you find that out? You didn't go out while I was gone, did you? I've told you, you have to be more careful—you've almost been spotted a dozen times."

"I have my ways," Kate said, still smiling. But then the smile faded. "But this can't go on much longer, Sterling. Jake is in so much trouble, he needs all the support he can get. This whole mess with Monica's murder, and waiting for the police or that investigator of Rebecca's to turn up the real killer, is bad enough, but to find out...the truth about his father on top of everything... My plans were to stay dead until I could figure out who tried to kill me. Well, now we know who it was, and she's dead. And my family needs me more than ever. I just have to figure out *how* to come back from the dead without killing them with the shock!''

"We'll talk about that later," the white-haired lawyer said rather gruffly as he embraced Kate gently.

Kate sighed. She'd come to rely so much on Sterling's crusty but unfailing support; she truly didn't know what she would have done without him. The Fortunes needed his wise counsel if they were to survive this debacle.

And they had to survive. She would not let it be otherwise. And whatever Fate had brought them to this pass would soon learn that Kate Fortune wasn't down yet.

The Fortunes, she thought determinedly, were not fate's children, but her children. And she would see them through.

*   *   *   *   *

FORTUNE'S CHILDREN

continues with

FORGOTTEN HONEYMOON

by Marie Ferrarella

Available in May

Here's an exciting preview....

Forgotten Honeymoon

"Hey, Max! It's for you."

Max Cooper turned toward his partner, who was waving a telephone receiver.

With a sigh, Max took off his hard hat and ran his hand through his unruly dark brown hair. He sincerely hoped that this wasn't someone calling about yet another delay. The construction of the housing development was already behind schedule.

Every time the phone rang, he mentally winced, anticipating another disaster.

Warily, Max put the receiver to his ear. "Hello?"

"Max? It's June," the anxious voice on the other end of the line said. "I hate bothering you, but you'd better come out here. You're going to want to see this."

June Cunningham was the receptionist at the Dew Drop Inn, the small bed-and-breakfast in which Max had inherited half interest from his foster parents.

"This?" he repeated.

"Ms. Fortune."

It was a minute before he reacted. "Kate? She's dead. She's been gone for nearly two years." Her lawyer, Sterling Foster, had sent him a letter saying probate would take a long time, considering the size of Kate's estate, so Max should continue to run the inn as always. But now it seemed there would be some changes.

"Not Kate," June quickly corrected. "Her heir. Kristina Fortune."

"She's there?"

"She's here, all right." He heard June stifle a sigh. "And she wants to meet you. Immediately."

"Immediately?"

June lowered her voice, as if afraid of being overheard. "Her word, not mine. But I really think you should get here, Max. I heard her murmuring something about knocking walls out."

That caught his attention. Just who the hell did this Kristina Fortune think she was?

"I'll be there as soon as I can."

It had possibilities.

Stepping away from the taxi she had taken at the airport, Kristina slowly approached the inn. With a good, solid effort, the inn could be transformed into a moneymaker.

Kristina had plans. Why just one bed-and-breakfast inn? Why not a chain? A chain that catered to the romantic in everyone. If she could make it work here, she could acquire small, quaint inns throughout the country and transform them into a string of Honeymoon Hideaways.

Her mood altered abruptly as she stumbled. Her three-inch heel had gotten caught in a crack in the wooden floor. Kristina frowned as she freed her heel. Someone should have fixed that.

Fixed was the operative word, she thought as she went on to examine the rest of the ground floor, finally returning to the front room where she'd begun. The woman who had introduced herself as June had remained with her almost the entire time. She wasn't much of a sounding board, preferring, instead, to point out the inn's "charm." It seemed that around here, "neglect" was synonymous with "charm."

Kristina raised her eyes to June's face when she heard the audible sigh of relief.

Pausing in her notes, Kristina turned to see who had arrived.

June pulled the newcomer over to the side. "Max, she wants to change things. Do something."

Slowly, Kristina's eyes took measure of the other half owner from head to foot. There was a lot to measure. Max Cooper looked, in Kristina's estimation, like a rangy cowboy who had taken the wrong turn at the last roundup. He was wearing worn jeans that adhered to his frame with a familiarity reserved for a lover.

Even at a distance, she saw his eyes were a very potent blue.

The man's appearance might have impressed someone from central casting, as well as a good handful of her female friends, but it didn't impress her.

Business sense impressed her, and he apparently didn't have any.

She was looking him over as if he was a piece of merchandise to be appraised, Max thought. He did his own appraising.

"Max, this is the new half owner." Kristina heard the way the woman emphasized the word *half.* June's smile deepened.

Not waiting to be introduced, Kristina stepped forward, thrusting her hand into Max's. "Kristina Fortune, Kate's granddaughter. At least, one of them," she amended, thinking of her half sister and cousins.

Max had the distinct impression that she was only partially here. Which was fine with him. He'd like it even better if none of her were here. June and the others did a fair job of maintaining the old place and he firmly believed in the old adage that if it wasn't broken, it shouldn't be fixed.

"Sorry, I was just thinking of my plan for the inn. We're turning it into a Honeymoon Hideaway." She watched his expression to see if he liked the name. He didn't.

Kristina paused and blew out a breath. Since he was the other owner, she supposed she had better explain it to him, even though she hated explaining herself. She preferred doing and letting others see for themselves.

"I guess I'm getting ahead of myself."

Now, there was an understatement. "Is this something you just made up?"

Kristina sighed. She was trying to hold on to her temper, but he wasn't making it easy. "If you're going to challenge everything I say, Cooper, we're not going to get anywhere."

He took a moment to compose himself. "What makes you think I want to get anywhere with you, Ms. Fortune? I like the inn just as it is."

He might, but what he wanted didn't count.

"Not good enough anymore." She ran a testing hand along the upholstery of a couch. "I'm half owner now."

He read her intentions loud and clear. Very deliberately he removed her hand from the sofa. "I own the other half. And you can't do anything without me."

But *can't* had never been part of Kristina's vocabulary.

MIRA Books is proud to present
the newest blockbuster from

DEBBIE MACOMBER

*"If I want to get married and have a family
(and I do!) it's time for a plan! Starting now."*

—Excerpt from Hallie McCarthy's diary

This Matter of Marriage

The Problem. Hallie's biological clock is ticking, she's
hitting the big three-0 and there's not one prospect for
marriage in sight.

Being an organized, goal-setting kind of person, however,
Hallie has...

The Solution. One full year to meet Mr. Right, her Knight in
Shining Armor.

But the dating game is always the same. One disaster after
another. Fortunately, Hallie can compare notes with her
neighbor, Steve Marris. He's divorced and in the same boat.
Hmm...too bad Hallie and Steve aren't interested in each other!

Available in April 1997 at your favorite retail outlet.

MIRA The brightest star in women's fiction

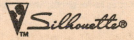

In April 1997
Bestselling Author

DALLAS SCHULZE

takes her Family Circle series to new heights with

In April 1997 Dallas Schulze brings readers a
brand-new, longer, out-of-series title featuring the
characters from her popular Family Circle miniseries.

When rancher Keefe Walker found Tessa Wyndham he
knew that she needed a man's protection—she was
pregnant, alone and on the run from a heartless past.
Keefe was also hiding from a dark past...but in one
overwhelming moment he and Tessa forged a family
bond that could never be broken.

Available in April wherever books are sold.

IN CELEBRATION OF MOTHER'S DAY, JOIN
SILHOUETTE THIS MAY AS WE BRING YOU

a funny thing
HAPPENED ON THE WAY TO THE
DELIVERY ROOM

THESE THREE STORIES, CELEBRATING THE
LIGHTER SIDE OF MOTHERHOOD, ARE
WRITTEN BY YOUR FAVORITE AUTHORS:

KASEY MICHAELS
KATHLEEN EAGLE
EMILIE RICHARDS

When three couples make the trip to the delivery
room, they get more than their own bundles of
joy…they get the promise of love!

Available this May,
wherever Silhouette books are sold.